Praise

"Sexy and wildly romantic."
—on *Doing Ireland!*

"Fully developed characters and perfect pacing
make this story feel completely right."
—on *Your Bed or Mine?*

"A very hot story mixes with great characters to
make every page a delight."
—on *The Mighty Quinns: Ian*

"Romantic, sexy and heartwarming."
—on *Who Needs Mistletoe?*

"Sexy, heartwarming and romantic...a story to
settle down with and enjoy—and then reread."
—on *The Mighty Quinns: Teague*

Dear Reader,

When I began the SMOOTH OPERATORS trilogy,
I was looking forward to writing three books set in
three different seasons—winter, spring and summer.
But with my writing schedule, I never seem to be
writing the books in the right season.

The first book of this trilogy, set in a snowbound
cabin, was written during the heat of August. This
book takes place in the Colorado springtime and
was written as the leaves were turning. And the
next book, set in Chicago in the summer, will no
doubt be written while the snow is flying. I guess
you could say I'm seasonally challenged.

Whatever the season, I find the escape of writing
just as much fun as a vacation. So enjoy this trip to
Boulder, Colorado. I've been there only once, but it
was a great place to visit.

Happy reading,

Kate Hoffmann

Kate Hoffmann

THE DRIFTER

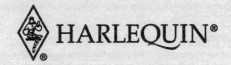

HARLEQUIN®

TORONTO • NEW YORK • LONDON
AMSTERDAM • PARIS • SYDNEY • HAMBURG
STOCKHOLM • ATHENS • TOKYO • MILAN • MADRID
PRAGUE • WARSAW • BUDAPEST • AUCKLAND

Recycling programs
for this product may
not exist in your area.

ISBN-13: 978-0-373-79536-9

THE DRIFTER

Copyright © 2010 by Peggy A. Hoffmann.

ABOUT THE AUTHOR

Kate Hoffmann began writing for Harlequin Books in 1993. Since then she's published sixty novels, primarily in the Harlequin Temptation and Harlequin Blaze lines. When she isn't writing, she enjoys music, theater and musical theater. She is active working with high school students in the performing arts. She lives in southeastern Wisconsin with her two cats, Chloe and Tally.

Books by Kate Hoffmann

HARLEQUIN BLAZE

HARLEQUIN TEMPTATION

HARLEQUIN SINGLE TITLES
(The Quinns)

For my ever-patient editor, Brenda Chin.

Prologue

"IT'S GOT TO BE SIMPLE and concise," Angela Weatherby said as she slowly twirled around in her desk chair. "The name has to encompass all the traits that make up this guy. He's a wanderer, he can't settle down. He's always searching for the next big thrill, whether it's climbing a mountain or seducing a beautiful woman. He freely admits that he doesn't want to commit, yet women fall for him again and again and again."

Now that her SmoothOperators Web site was such a success, Angela had found it much easier to work on the book she was writing. She'd chosen a title— Spotting the Smooth Operator: A Woman's Guide to Avoiding Dating Disasters. She'd developed ten solid archetypes of the smooth operator. But, according to her editor, she needed to come up with clever names for each. The chapter on the Charmer had already been written and she'd moved on to the next in line, then become stuck on the header.

"So he's a wanderer," said Celia Peralto, Angie's business partner and webmaster. "A…nomad?"

"That makes him sound like he's tending sheep instead of seducing women. How about the Traveler?"

Celia shook her head. "Sounds like some stuffy businessman."

A long silence grew between them. Ceci had been an invaluable help on the book and was always happy to brainstorm ideas. But this one had them both stumped. "It's on the tip of my tongue," Angela said. "He's a…a…" She groaned and closed her eyes, clearing her mind. "He's a—drifter!"

She opened her eyes to find Ceci grinning at her. "That's it," Ceci said. "He's a drifter. I like it. He can't settle down, he moves from one woman to the next, he's footloose and irresponsible and every woman thinks she'll be the one to change him."

"But no one can," Angela said.

"Well, there's always an exception to the rule," Ceci said. "If there wasn't, there would be a bunch of eighty-year old guys hopping from bed to bed, seducing any woman they could find." She paused. "There was a post on the Web site this morning. Alex Stamos has officially stepped out of the dating pool. His sister added a note to his profile saying that he's getting married."

"Well, it's good I never got to interview him, then," Angela said.

When she'd decided to do anonymous and anecdotal interviews with each of her "types," Alex had been first on her list. He'd been the perfect example of a "Charmer." Unfortunately, she'd never been able to talk to him and had to settle for a car salesman from Arlington Heights and a bartender from DePaul.

"You don't believe men can change, do you?" Ceci asked.

"I used to think they could," Angela admitted. "But how many profiles do we have on the site? Tens of thousands and yet, only a few men make the transformation from smooth operator to devoted husband. I've had just enough bad experiences to make me cynical."

"Don't you hope that someday you'll find a great guy, someone who won't treat you like a commodity?"

Angela sighed. In her heart of hearts, she still wanted to believe there was someone out there for her. But she was slowly creeping toward thirty and she knew the odds. The older she got, the smaller the bachelor pool became, until all that was left in the water were the bottom feeders and leeches and poisonous snakes. She was a practical girl who had let go of her fairy-tale dreams a long time ago.

"Of course I do," Angela murmured. "But I'm not going to hold my breath."

"A more optimistic attitude might help," Celia said. She crawled out of her chair and pulled Angela to her feet. "Go ahead. Close your eyes, click your heels together and say it three times. I will fall in love with a great man, I will fall in love with a great man, I will fall in love with a great man."

Angela laughed and pulled her hands out of Ceci's grip. "You're a hopeless romantic. How can you do your job and not see that finding a good guy is like looking for diamond in a pile of dipsticks?"

Ceci sighed. "All right. Maybe it's better you hate men, at least until this book is done."

"I don't hate men."

Reaching across her desk, Ceci snatched up a magazine and tossed it at Angela. "You wanted to interview a drifter?" She pointed to the picture on the cover of *Outdoor Adventure* magazine. "Charlie Templeton. He has a huge profile on our site. And he is a classic example. He's doing a couple lectures at the university in Boulder, Colorado. I figure you could fly out there, corner him and get him to talk."

Angela peered at the photo. "God, he is gorgeous."

"He is," Ceci said. "Of course, if you'd rather, I could fly out there and interview him."

"No. I'll do it. If I surprise him, maybe he'll agree to talk."

Angela set the magazine down, then went back to scanning the newest profiles created on the Web site. Who would have known that a silly little blog chronicling her dating woes would have turned into a thriving business? She ought to be grateful to every guy who ever dumped her for giving her the opportunity of a lifetime.

There was one chapter she wasn't ready to write, though. One that brought up all sorts of memories. She needed time to prepare for her memories of Max Morgan, the Sexy Devil. Time to work up the courage to call him for an interview. Would he even remember her?

All through high school, she'd had a secret crush on him and he'd never once noticed her. He'd been the most popular guy, the star athlete, the boy every girl dreamed of kissing. She'd followed him to college at Northwestern, attending all his football and baseball games, taking every opportunity to put herself in his path. Looking back on it, her behavior probably could have been considered stalking.

"Do you want me to make reservations?" Ceci asked.

"What? Oh, for Boulder? Yes. And do the hotel, too. Do that thing you do when you get the really good rates. If Charlie Templeton won't talk, I don't want to regret wasting money on a nice hotel room."

She hadn't been able to snag Alex Stamos, but she'd learned from her mistakes. The best way to catch a smooth operator was to eliminate any means of escape. They called it ambush journalism, but Angela preferred to think of it as just a way to get the job done.

1

CHARLIE TEMPLETON STOOD at the top of the world. Literally. He sucked in a deep breath from the oxygen mask covering his face. The air was thin at 28,740 feet and after climbing for nearly twelve hours, all he really wanted to do was lie down and sleep. But he knew the risks of taking just a moment or two of relaxation. Many climbers had died ascending Mount Everest, but the descent was even trickier.

Exhausted, his body depleted of energy reserves, cold, hungry and mentally numb, Charlie knew all the dangers. The thought of dying on the face of the world's tallest mountain had haunted his nightmares. But now that he was here, it didn't seem all that frightening. He closed his eyes and let his thoughts drift. Just a moment was all he needed.

Everest was the last on his list of seven summits. He'd attempted the climb twice in the past, but had been forced to stop because of weather. But when he'd stepped out his tent at midnight, ready for the final push to the top, he'd known today would be the day.

For an adventurer, there was no higher goal than bagging the seven summits—the tallest peak on each continent. He'd written about his quest for the adventure Web site Adrenaline and had done numerous speaking engagements at college campuses all over the U.S., all to fund his trips. He had a pair of lectures scheduled in just a few weeks at the university in his hometown of Boulder and he was banking on the fact that he'd arrive fresh off the top of Everest, ready to tell of his adventure.

But now that he'd accomplished his goal, Charlie was left to wonder what it all meant. He didn't feel the way he'd expected—elated, awestruck, satisfied, humbled. In truth, Charlie didn't feel anything.

He unsnapped his oxygen mask and pushed it aside, then shoved his goggles to the top of his head, taking in the view and waiting for the impact of the moment to hit him. It was all there, more stunning than he'd ever imagined it. Below him was the Rongbuck glacier and the North Col, and to the north horizon, the vast Tibetan plateau. He slowly turned, to the west and then the south, finishing with the most breathtaking view of all—the highest peaks of the Himalayas, jagged and snow-covered, jutting into the thin atmosphere to the east.

He closed his eyes and drew a deep breath. An

image flashed in his brain and he gasped. A face from the past. Charlie brushed it aside. God, he must really be oxygen-deprived to think of her at a time like this. He hadn't spoken to Eve Keller in more than five years, not since the night before he departed for his first attempt at Everest.

Maybe that was it. He'd completed the circle and he was back to where he'd begun. Or was it something more? Charlie had learned to live his life without regrets. It wasn't easy, but he'd had to put aside relationships in order to focus on his ambitions. It hadn't seemed like a sacrifice at the time, but now that he'd come to the end of his quest, he had to wonder if it had all been worth it.

"Evie," he murmured. She'd been the one person who'd tempted him, the one relationship that might have changed the course of his life. Hell, if he'd stayed with her, he'd probably be married with two or three kids by now.

"Charlie!" He opened his eyes to find his Sherpa guide waving at him. "Come. Up here long enough. We start down."

"Just give me a few more minutes," Charlie replied.

"Put mask back on," Pemba Ang said, his heavily accented words muffled by his oxygen mask.

"No. It gets in the way. I'm all right. I am. Don't worry. Just a few more minutes."

The guide studied him for a long moment, then

nodded. "Few minutes. Stay up here for half hour already. We must go."

Had it been that long? Time seemed to be slipping through his fingers at an alarming rate. It seemed like just days ago that he'd graduated college and now he was fast approaching thirty.

Charlie turned again, slowly, taking in more of the view. It was over. He was finally finished. He had the rest of his life in front of him and no plans for how he'd spend it. Why hadn't he thought of this sooner? What would he do with his time? There was always the "Second Seven," the second-highest peaks on each continent. But was he willing to invest another five years of his life?

"Charlie!"

The words echoed in his ears. But in the thin air, it didn't sound like Ang at all. It sounded sweet and soft, tantalizing. Funny how he still remembered her voice. There'd been so many other women since Eve, women he'd easily forgotten. Yet she was still there, indelibly imprinted into his brain.

Charlie stared down the route of their descent, his footprints still visible in the snow. He still had to get down the mountain and he knew the dangers. Fatigue, the weather, cerebral edema, snow blindness, avalanches, crevices that could swallow a man in the blink of an eye. A successful ascent didn't guarantee a safe descent. But what was waiting for him at the bottom? Would anyone really care that he'd made it up to the top and back again?

Did she even remember him? Did she think of him at all or had the passion they'd shared been replaced by the love she felt for…hell, what was his name? Dave? Dan? Odd that he couldn't remember. She'd married him, chosen security and dependability over uncertainty. He hadn't blamed her for making the safe choice. She deserved better than a man who warmed her bed every six months in between adventures.

"Charlie! Move. We head down."

"I'm thinking I might stay here," he said, sitting down in the snow.

"Get ass up!" Ang shouted, grabbing his arm and tugging. "I not leave you here. You walk down or I carry. Kill us both."

"Who's waiting for you?" Charlie asked.

Ang reached for Charlie's oxygen bottle and turned up the flow, then held the mask over his face. "Breathe. Clear head."

"I'm perfectly clear," Charlie said, waving him off. "Do you have a wife, kids?"

"Wife," Ang muttered. "We marry last year."

"And she's all right with this? She doesn't mind that you tramp up and down Mount Everest."

"This my last trip. We have baby. I tell wife, no more. I save money from many climbs, we open laundry in Namche. We have happy life. Grow old together." He held out his arm and pointed to his watch, strapped over his sleeve. "See? We leave now. You move or I roll you down to base camp."

"No one would care if I didn't make it down," Charlie said.

"I would," Ang said. "I never lose client." He helped Charlie to his feet. "Maybe, you need wife. Someone who care. Maybe kids. Can't do that frozen to mountain. You go find happy. Find girl you love."

"No," Charlie said. "I think I had her once, but I let her go."

"Two years back, I love my girl. Another man love her, too. I make her see we have happy life together. All is well."

For an instant, Charlie's mind cleared. What *was* to stop him? Maybe that's what he needed to do. Go back and figure out if he had made the wrong choice that night five years ago. And if he had, try to fix it. Suddenly, he had a reason to get down the mountain. He'd go see Eve. He'd figure out why it was her face he'd seen.

"All right," Charlie said, clapping Ang's shoulder. "Let's get off this damn mountain." He snapped his oxygen mask back in place and pulled his goggles down over his eyes.

In a week's time, he could be back in Boulder, Colorado. Back where it all began. Then maybe he'd figure out what he was supposed to do with the rest of his life.

"LONELY GUY AT TABLE SEVEN. And he's a hottie!"

Eve Keller glanced over her shoulder at her best friend and business partner, Lily Winston, then shook her head. "In case you haven't heard, the Garden Gate is one of the best restaurants in Boulder according to a recent article in the Denver Post."

"Oh, yes," Lily teased. "But I hear the chef at the Garden Gate is turning into a bit of diva. Television appearances, interviews in foodie magazines, a new cookbook and a possible television series for the Food Channel. Her partner has been having trouble finding toques that fit her ever-expanding head. Of course, she can't be bothered with something as mundane as a handsome man."

"One of the reasons we've been successful is that we focus on outstanding food and impeccable service. Not hitting on the customers," Eve said.

"I'm not looking to date him," Lily said. "I'm perfectly happy with Will. I'm just looking to...look. God, he's gorgeous. You should go out there and ask him if he likes his curried carrot soup."

Eve groaned. Since her divorce three years ago, she hadn't put much effort into dating. In truth, she'd put more thought into becoming a NASA astronaut than she had searching for a new man. Not that she didn't have a perfectly valid excuse for living like a nun. Her restaurant was growing in popularity. She'd already published one vegetarian cookbook and was working on another. Add to that the seminars she taught at three different cooking schools on the West Coast and there wasn't much time for a social life. She was even in preliminary talks with an investment group about opening a new restaurant in Seattle and hosting a cable show on the Food Channel.

Men had simply drifted to the bottom of the list of important things on her agenda. After the mess that had been her marriage and the bigger mess that had been her divorce, Eve wasn't sure she ever wanted to allow a man into her life again.

"Just take a look," Lily said, pulling Eve away from the prep table. "You've been living in my guest room for three years. I see your social life first hand and it's pathetic. Last week you alphabetized the spices on my spice rack. The week before, you cleaned the grease trap on the kitchen sink. You need to get a life, Eve."

"I have a life. Here. In this restaurant."

"This isn't life. It's work." Lily gently took the knife from her hand and set it next to the red peppers Eve had been chopping. Then she reached up and snatched the colorful bandanna off Eve's head. "Go ahead," she said, ruffling Eve's short-cropped auburn hair. "Just wander on out there, smile at the customers, and ask him how his soup is." Lily shoved a basket of quick breads into her hand. "Offer him some three-grain nut loaf."

Eve knew she ought to spend more time in the dining room. All the best chefs interacted with their clientele. But life inside the confines of the kitchen was so much easier than life in the outside world. She peeked though the window of the swinging door, searching for the object of Lily's attention.

When her gaze finally found the lonely guy at table seven, her breath caught in her throat. "Oh, God," she muttered, turning away from the door.

"You don't think he's cute?" Lily asked. "Oh, good grief, Eve, if you're that picky you're never going to have sex again for the rest of your life."

"Yes, he's cute," Eve snapped. "But I'm not going out there."

"Why?" Lily asked, taking a peek through the window. "Too cute?"

"Too...everything," Eve said, shoving the basket back into Lily's hands. "Been there, done that."

Lily gasped. "You know him?"

Eve nodded. "Unfortunately, yes. In every sense of the word. I have seen him naked and trust me, the body matches the face. Utterly and unbelievably gorgeous." A shiver skittered down her spine at the memory. There'd been a time when she'd had that body in her bed, lying on her sofa, standing in front of his refrigerator looking for something to eat at three in the morning.

"But...I don't understand."

Eve took Lily's arm and led her over to the walk-in fridge, then pulled open the door. "Go ahead. I'm not going to spill my secrets unless we have complete privacy." They stepped inside and Eve closed the door behind her.

Lily rubbed her bare arms. "If this is going to be a long story, I'm going to need a jacket."

"Remember that night, after we got the good review in *Food and Wine,* and we drank those two bottles of Mendocino Monastery Reserve Cabernet? And I told you about that guy, the one right before I married Matt?"

"The 'one last fling' guy?" Lily asked. "That's him?"

Eve nodded. "Charlie Templeton."

"You dumped *him* for Matt?" Lily stared at her as if she'd just admitted to serving puppy fritters with kitten aioli to the customers. "Dweeby, whiny, needy Matt?"

"I didn't know he was like that when I married him. He seemed—dependable. It was only after the wedding I realized he was looking for a mother, not a wife. And Charlie was everything a girl is supposed to be afraid of. After a month of nonstop sex, he told me he was going to be gone for six months. At the time, I needed a man who'd be there for more than a bi-annual sexfest."

"Semi-annual," Lily corrected. "And now he's back."

"Five years later. *Five* years and not a word. No phone call, no postcard. Now can you understand my decision?"

"Why do you think he came back?"

Eve had a niggling suspicion. In truth, she wasn't proud of what she'd done. And it had come after another very expensive bottle of wine and an evening of feeling sorry for herself. She'd happened upon a Web site called SmoothOperators.com, a place where women could off-load all their dating horror stories. She'd been so fed up with men that night, she'd created a profile for every bad date she'd ever been on, full of all the tiny details describing the men who'd done her wrong. And Charlie Templeton had been at the top of the list. In many ways, she blamed him for her bad marriage and painful divorce.

Had he stayed, maybe just a few days more, even a week, she might have realized that marrying Matt was the wrong choice. She would have come to understand that passion was much more important than security.

"It could just be coincidence," Eve murmured. "The last time he was here, I was just head chef. He doesn't know I own the restaurant now."

"Or maybe he does and he's come to see you. You won't know unless you go out there and talk to him."

A knock sounded on the walk-in door. Lily grabbed the handle and opened the door. "We're almost done," she called.

Eve saw Sarah, their best waitress, standing outside and she stepped around Lily. "We are done," she said. "What do you need?"

"There's a gentleman at table seven who'd like to speak to the chef. I think he might know you."

"See," Lily said. "I told you he came here for a reason." She grabbed Eve's arm and steered her out the door. "Fluff up your hair, you still have hat head. And put on a fresh jacket. On second thought, don't wear the jacket."

Lily reached for the buttons and Eve slapped her hands away. "Have you been spending time with my mother? Because you're beginning to sound exactly like her."

She slipped out of her jacket and tossed it over a stool at the prep table, then ran her fingers through her short-cropped hair. For the first time since her divorce, she regretted not paying more attention to her make-up and wardrobe. Eve had always relied on her natural beauty to get by. So much for taking Charlie's breath away.

Gathering her resolve, she pushed on the swinging door and stepped out into the dining room. The Garden Gate was a different restaurant during the daylight hours. Sheets of butcher paper replaced the linen tablecloths. A mish-mash of colorful ceramic stoneware stood in for the more elegant and refined china and crystal they used for the dinner crowd.

He looked up as she approached and her breath caught in her throat. She'd never forgotten those eyes, pale blue and penetrating, as if he could see right inside her soul. And that hair, thick and wavy and streaked by the sun. He was dressed casually, in a faded polo shirt and cargo pants.

Eve pasted a smile on her face. It wouldn't do to seem rattled by his appearance. She'd treat him like any other customer. But try as she might, Eve couldn't forget that this was a customer who had once made her moan with pleasure, who had taken her to places she'd never been sexually. She drew a shaky breath. "Hello, Charlie."

He stood, dropping his napkin on the table. "Hi, Eve." Before she could react, he stepped toward her and placed a kiss on her cheek, his fingers skimming down her bare arm. "It's good to see you."

Eve's heart slammed her chest and she glanced down at the spot where his fingers had made contact. For a long moment, she couldn't think of a single thing to say. Then she blurted out the first thing that came to mind. "Look at that. You're out of water. I'll go get you another glass."

When she reached the safety of the kitchen, Eve headed right back to the walk-in fridge, ignoring the curious glances of the kitchen staff before slamming the door behind her. She sat down on a crate of potatoes and buried her face in her hands. After all this time, he still had the ability to make her pulse race and her head spin.

How many times had she thought of him over the

past five years? As her marriage had deteriorated, he'd come to mind more and more often. She'd been left to wonder whether incredible sex twice a year might have been better than a husband who'd cheated on her with a series of college co-eds.

Her choice to marry Matt had been the biggest mistake of her life. In truth, she hoped that by accepting Matt's proposal, Charlie might make a counteroffer. When he didn't, she decided that Matt was a reasonable alternative. Though they didn't share a wild, uncontrollable desire for each other, she and Matt shared the same goals—buying their own restaurant and turning Eve Keller into a household name.

When a knock sounded on the fridge door, Eve pushed to her feet. "I'm done," she called. "Come on in."

The door opened and to Eve's astonishment, Charlie stepped inside, holding an empty glass. "I'm sorry, but I was getting really thirsty out there and you said you were bringing me water and I—" He closed the door and leaned back against it. Slowly, he took a deep breath, then let it out, the air clouding in front of his face. "You're more beautiful than I remembered, Evie."

Eve stiffened her spine. Evie. A tremor rocked her body and she rubbed her arms. She remembered how he'd whispered her name as he moved inside of her, his voice inviting her to join him. Come on, Evie. Come with me. Let go.

"What are you doing here? It's been five years without a word. And now you show up and expect me to fall for that cheesy line?"

He glanced around and chuckled. "That's right. You don't serve cheese in this restaurant."

"Actually, we do. We went from strict vegan to organic vegetarian when I bought the restaurant. And on weekends we also serve fish and seafood."

"I'll keep that in mind the next time I try to pay you a compliment." He stepped toward her. "I just wanted to stop by and say hello. And let you know that I've been thinking of you."

"Of me?" she asked. "Or of a warm body to spend the next month in your bed?" Eve turned and began to rearrange the cheese on the shelf in front of her. "I'm not going to fall for that again," she said, waving a wedge of Camembert at him.

"Are you angry with me?" Charlie asked. "Because, as I recall, you made the choice to marry Dan. Or Dave."

"Matt. His name was Matt."

"Was? What, did he get hit by a bus while I was gone?"

She scowled. "Is!"

"You said was. Past tense. Now, either he met with some unfortunate accident or you're no longer married to him. Which is it, Evie?"

"Stop calling me that! And it's none of your business!" she snapped. She walked past him on wobbly legs, but he quickly stepped in front of her to block her escape. She took a deep breath, trying to still her body's trembling. "Why are you here? If it's about the Web site, I was—"

"What Web site?"

She risked a glance up at him. "Never mind. I meant—"

He reached out and smoothed his hand over her cheek. Then, before Eve could continue, he bent close and dropped a kiss on her lips. As if that weren't nearly enough, he kissed her again, this time, more purposefully.

His tongue gently tasted and Eve parted her lips and let him delve more deeply. Her body felt boneless, weak and lacking any power to resist him. Charlie knew how to kiss a woman. And he knew exactly how to kiss her. She slipped her arms around his neck and pressed her body against his, aching for his warmth and willing to enjoy the moment while it lasted.

Eve didn't care what had brought him back to her. In truth, she didn't even care if he was about to walk out of her life for another five years. All she wanted was this kiss. She could live for a long time off just one kiss.

Since the divorce had been finalized two years ago, she'd avoided men. But now that one had presented himself, Eve realized how much she'd been missing. She loved the feel of a man's body, the warmth and the strength, the scent of his cologne, the sensation of his hair slipping through her fingers. And then there was the delicious wash of desire that raced through her at his touch.

Was it just Charlie? Or would she have had this reaction to any man? When he finally drew back, Eve opened her eyes and looked up to find a bemused smile twitching at his lips. "I was right," he murmured. "It's not finished, is it?"

"What?"

"I have to go," Charlie said. "I'll be back, though."

Eve gasped. Was this some kind of test? "When? A year from now? Five years? Don't think you can just waltz in here and kiss me and—"

He grabbed her around the waist and kissed her again, effectively stopping her outburst. "Later. Tonight. Right now, I have some important things to do." With that, he turned and slipped out the door.

Eve stared out into the kitchen. The staff was assembled around the prep table, watching her with curious gazes. "He's an old friend," Eve explained. "He just stopped by to say hello." She rolled her eyes. "Just get back to work."

She hurried out of the walk-in and snatched up her jacket. As she slipped her arms through the starched white sleeves, Eve thought about all that had happened in the past ten minutes. Her life had been right on track, everything in perfect order, and then, in the blink of an eye, it had all changed.

If it hadn't been her posting on the SmoothOperators Web site, what had brought him back to Boulder? Would it be foolish to think he came back just to see her? Eve shook her head and picked up her knife.

What did it matter? Charlie Templeton wasn't the type to want a traditional relationship—a marriage, a house, a family. No matter what transpired over the next few days, he'd be gone again and she'd be alone, left to carry on as if nothing happened.

Eve set the knife down, pausing to let the notion sink in. Five years ago, she had looked upon that possibility as a negative. But now, Eve had to admit that it might just be exactly what she needed. A wild and exciting sexual affair with no strings attached.

The possibility of falling in love again frightened her. She'd made two mistakes—falling for Charlie in the first place and deluding herself into believing that she loved Matt. Three strikes and she'd be out, unable to trust anyone for the rest of her life. If she fell in love again, it would have to be with a man who wouldn't hurt her.

Eve drew a deep breath and let it out slowly. She had tried so hard to avoid the mistakes that her parents had made with their marriage. Her father had cheated on her mother for as long as she could remember. And for almost as long, her mother had been aware of what he'd been doing and had just looked the other way.

Charlie had been the wrong choice. Matt had been the wrong choice. Until the right choice came along, she wasn't going to risk her heart again. She paused. But what if she kept her heart out it? What if she indulged in a purely sexual relationship with Charlie?

Eve smiled to herself. It was an option she ought to consider. Two years was far too long to go without sex. But great sex every six months might be exactly enough. "I have a lot of catching up to do," she murmured to herself.

CHARLIE GLANCED AT HIS WATCH, illuminating the face to see the numerals in the dark.

"You keep looking at the time," Jack said. "Do you have somewhere you need to be?"

"Yeah," he said. "I've got a...a date."

His old friend chuckled then shook his head. "You've been in town for less than twenty-four hours and you already have a date. Jeez, you move fast."

"It's not like that," Charlie said. "She's an old friend. She runs a restaurant downtown and she finishes work at eleven. I'm going to stop by and invite her out for a drink."

After what had happened earlier that day, Charlie had decided to proceed slowly. Eve had made it clear that she still harbored a few grudges. And she had every right. He'd walked out of her life five years ago after an incredible month together, and then never called or wrote. On the other hand, she had decided to marry another man, so contact probably would have been inappropriate.

He'd been given a second chance. They were both single and he had some time on his hands. And he needed to know just where this all might lead. He wasn't going to mess it up by seducing her on the first date.

"And here, I thought you came back to town to see your old buddy Jack."

"Actually, I came back to Boulder to give a couple of lectures at the university. Seeing the girl again is just a bonus."

"How's your mom?"

"She's doing well," Charlie said. "Now that I'm home for a while, I'll have time to go out to visit her in San Diego. I called her this morning. She was glad to hear the seven summits was done. I stopped telling her about the climbs until after they were through. She worries too much."

"You always were a thrill junkie," Jack said. "My son is like that. Last summer, he jumped off the garage roof into our swimming pool. I didn't know what to do. He was so proud of himself."

"How old is he?" Charlie asked.

"Eight," Jack said.

It was hard to believe that Jack had a eight-year-old son, or that he'd been married nearly ten years. He and Jack had been friends since their freshman year at UC. Charlie had left Boulder after graduation, but Jack had stuck around to get his masters and then a doctorate. Now he taught mathematics at the university. "Could you stand another beer?" Charlie asked. "I don't have to leave yet."

He pushed to his feet and walked into the house. The interior of the three-bedroom bungalow brought back a flood of memories from his childhood. The last time he was in Boulder, he'd come to help his widowed mom get packed up to make her move to San Diego, to a condo near his sister's place. He'd decided to buy the house from her and she'd given him an outrageously low price, considering the real-estate market in Boulder.

He'd intended to fix up the house and sell it, but he'd never gotten around to calling an agent. He'd met Evie and spent an entire month in bed with her. Had he known, somewhere deep inside, that he'd be back someday? That he'd want and need a place to call home?

Most of his belongings were scattered around the country, some in the attic here in Boulder, some in Chicago with his brother, and the rest in his mother's storage locker at her condo. He lived out of a back-pack and didn't possess a single item larger than the rear cargo area of his ten-year-old Jeep.

This was the only place that felt like home. After

his father had died when he was ten, his mother had been forced to sell the big house they'd lived in and rented the ramshackle bungalow on Tenth Street. Without any source of income, she'd gone back to school and got a teaching degree, while Charlie and his two younger siblings were left to fend for themselves. She'd scraped together enough to buy the home from their generous landlord and lived there until the last of her children had graduated from UC.

His sister worked at a large advertising agency in San Diego and his brother was a trader in downtown Chicago. Charlie's profession, on the other hand, was best described as an adventurer-slash-writer. An after-school program in rock climbing had led to his interest in outdoor adventure and living in Boulder gave him plenty of opportunities to hone his skills as a climber.

Charlie snagged a few beers from the fridge, then grabbed a bag of chips he'd bought on a quick trip to the grocery store. Though the house had been shut up since the renters left six months ago, the cool breeze blowing through the open windows had carried away the last traces of musty air.

When he got back to the porch, he handed Jack a beer, then sat down on the plastic chair, kicking his feet back up on the porch railing. "Thanks for taking care of the house."

"I thought you were planning to sell it."

"I was. But it never seemed like the right time."

"It's kind of silly to keep it," Jack said. "You're never here. And it's probably worth close to a million if you'd fix it up a little bit."

Charlie shrugged. "I'm thinking of staying for a while. I'll get a little work done around here, relax and—"

"Who is she?" Jack interrupted. "And what has she done to the Charlie Templeton I've always known."

"It's not like that. I've just been...reevaluating." He took a sip of his beer, wondering how much he wanted to reveal. Hell, he wasn't sure how he felt, but Charlie knew something had changed inside him. The circuit in his brain that had caused him to wander the world, searching for the next big thrill, had been switched off. "I was standing on top of Everest and I couldn't believe it."

"Man, that must have felt incredible."

That was the problem, Charlie mused. It hadn't felt incredible. But kissing Evie had. Just pulling her into his arms and feeling her warm, soft body against his had been...thrilling. Through all his adventures, he'd never felt that. Satisfaction, yes. Pride, of course. But nothing had matched that first kiss in the restaurant refrigerator.

"It didn't," Charlie said. "I'd achieved everything I'd ever wanted and it didn't make me happy."

"What are you, freakin' crazy? You get paid to do stuff I can only dream about. You have no responsibilities. You decide you want to go surfing in

Australia and you're there the next day. Jenny and I have been planning to go to Banff for nearly a year and we still haven't picked a date. Taking a family of four on a vacation is like planning a military invasion."

"But you like it, right? The wife, the family. It's all good?"

"Sure," Jack replied. "I'm not saying it's easy, or that every day is a disaster. Or that I don't envy you on those nights when the kids are sick or when Jenny is mad about something. But I don't know what I'd do if they weren't in my life."

"That's the thing," Charlie said, leaning forward and bracing his elbows on his knees. "You've got someone, someone who cares that you walk in the door at night."

"You have family," he said.

Charlie shook his head. "It's not the same. Family is required to love you. They don't have a choice. Besides, they consider me the black sheep in the family. The sibling who never quite grew up. I want someone who needs me."

"Jenny says men chase immortality. That's why we look at younger women, why we're afraid of commitment, why we get drunk and howl at the moon. She heard it in a movie and now, whenever I do something stupid, she says it's because I fear getting old."

Charlie frowned. "I don't think about getting old."

"Your dad died when he was thirty-six. You don't

ever think of that? I mean, you're going to be thirty next year, right?"

"Shit, you're right," he muttered. "And no, I really didn't think much about it until now."

"Maybe that's why you chase adventure," Jack said.

"What are you, my shrink?"

"No, but I watch a lot of Dr. Phil when the kids are home sick."

Charlie set his beer down and got to his feet. "I have to go."

"What time is it?" Jack asked. "I told Jenny I'd be home by ten."

"It's close to eleven."

Jack jumped up, wagging a finger at Charlie. "See, this is what I love about your life. I'm required to be in by ten and you're just going out at eleven. You know, hooking up with a girl this late at night looks suspiciously like a booty call."

Charlie frowned. "You think? I don't want to give her the wrong idea. I'm not expecting a hook-up. Maybe I should call first."

"That would make it worse," Jack said. "Just tell her you were out for a walk. That would play much better if you had a dog. You can come over and borrow our dog."

"You have a dog?"

"And two cats, a fluctuating number of fish, and a hamster that's been missing for three days."

Charlie found the news strangely disquieting. Jack really was settled. And as much as his friend couldn't imagine what climbing Everest was like, Charlie couldn't fathom caring for a family and a houseful of pets.

"The grass is always greener," Charlie murmured. They jogged down the porch steps together. "I'll stop by tomorrow and see the kids," he said. "Tell Jenny I'm sorry I kept you out so late."

They walked in opposite directions, Jack toward the family he had waiting and Charlie toward the unknown. Hell, he wasn't sure what he was doing in Boulder or why he was so intent on seeing Eve again. But he'd always allowed his instincts to rule his life and right now, this was where he was supposed to be.

The fifteen-minute walk to downtown Boulder was filled with indecision. Charlie was anxious to see Eve again, if only to find out whether the attraction they'd experienced earlier that day was more than one-sided.

This was really crazy. He'd always known exactly what he wanted in life, planning each move ahead of time and throwing all his energy into making a success of whatever he tried. But here he was, wandering the streets of his hometown, without a clue as to why he was here.

He'd never put much stock in psychiatry, but he had to wonder if something hadn't snapped in his brain when he was at high altitude. Lack of oxygen could do funny things to a guy's head, even make him feel something that wasn't really there.

His mind drifted back to the kiss, to the taste of her mouth, the way she opened beneath him. He'd felt something then, something powerful. He'd kissed a lot of women and relying on his experience, Charlie was pretty sure Evie had wanted to be kissed. She'd even enjoyed it. And before the night was over, he planned to do it again.

The restaurant was empty of customers when he arrived, though the front door was still open. He walked inside, catching the attention of a bartender who was stacking glasses behind the bar.

"Sorry, we're closed," he said.

"I know," Charlie replied. "I'm here to see Eve."

The bartender gave him a suspicious look. "Kind of late for a sales call."

"We're old friends. I was here earlier for lunch. I told her I'd stop by later."

The bartender nodded toward the kitchen door. "She's in back."

Charlie peeked through the small diamond-shaped window in the door. Eve had her back to him as she flipped through a sheaf of papers, separating them into piles on a wide stainless-steel table. He slowly pushed open the door.

"Kenny, can you bring up a case of the '96 Castle Ridge Merlot before you leave?"

"Just tell me where it is," Charlie said softly. He watched her spine stiffen before she slowly turned around. He held his breath, still taken aback by her beauty. What had he been thinking all those years ago? How had it been so easy to walk away from her?

"What are you doing here?"

He grinned. "I don't know. I thought I could walk you home."

"I drove," she said.

"So then maybe you can drive me home?"

"I still have a lot of work to do," she said.

Charlie let the door swing shut behind him, then crossed to the table. Boosting himself up, he sat next to her, studying her work. She seemed perturbed and he wondered at the cause. "I thought we could go out. Get a drink or maybe a cup of coffee?"

Eve drew in a deep breath, then turned to face him. "Why are you here?" Shaking her head, she held up her hand. "Never mind, I know the answer to that."

He chuckled. "You do? Good, then maybe you can tell me. Because I haven't figured it out yet." Charlie reached out and took her hand in his, distractedly playing with her fingers. He'd forgotten how soft her skin was. And how delicate her fingers were. All the little details that had faded over time now came rushing back. "How much longer do you have to work?"

The kitchen door swung open and Kenny poked

his head inside. Eve snatched her hand away. "I'm done," he said. "I locked the front doors."

"Thanks," Eve said, glancing over her shoulder. "I'll see you tomorrow night."

He gave Charlie another look, then shrugged. "Night, boss." Kenny strolled through the kitchen and out the back, the screen door slamming behind him.

Charlie slid off the table. "Where's that wine you needed?"

"Through that door, down the stairs, second shelf from the top on the right. Castle Ridge Merlot. The '96 Reserve. Bring up the rest of the case."

As he completed the task, Charlie wondered at her prickly attitude. Women usually warmed up right away when he turned on the charm. But then, he'd never gone back to one of his previous conquests. Though she had every right to be angry, she'd been the one to choose marriage over adventure, stability over spontaneity. Did she blame him for forcing her to make the wrong choice? He cursed softly. Or maybe she *did* assume he was only here for booty call.

When he got upstairs, he set the case on the opposite side of the table, then leaned over it, bracing his arms on the rough wood edges. "So, is this any good?" he asked, pulling a bottle and holding it out to her.

"Yes. It's very good."

"Then I'd like to buy a bottle. Do you have a couple of glasses and a corkscrew?"

"It's seventy-five dollars a bottle."

"Then I guess it better be good," Charlie replied.

She set her work down and stared at him. He waited for her to speak, but she seemed to be carefully considering what she was about to say. "Why are you here? If you've come for sex, why don't you just say so and stop wasting time with wine and pretty compliments." She smoothed her hands over the stainless-steel table. "We could do it right here and get it over with."

"You think that's what this is about? Have I even brought up sex?"

"No, but..."

"Odd that you'd mention it. Have you been thinking about it? I mean, sex with me?"

"Yes," she said. "No! Not in the way you think. I've just been wondering why you stopped by today."

"I think we better crack open this bottle of wine, because it's a long story. And a large quantity of alcohol would help in the telling."

Eve took the bottle from his hand, then searched through a nearby drawer for a corkscrew. She held it out to him, then fetched a pair of wineglasses from a plastic rack near the dishwasher. Slowly, she slid them in front of him and after removing the cork, he filled the glasses halfway.

"So what's the story?" she asked before taking a sip.

"First, a toast," he said, holding his glass up. "To old friends."

Eve touched her wine goblet to his, then took a sip. "Old friends," she repeated softly. "So what is the story?"

"Have you ever had an epiphany?" he asked. "A moment of absolute clarity in your life? When you know exactly who you are and what you're supposed to be doing?"

"No," she said.

"Neither have I. But I should have. I was standing on top of Everest, cold and hungry and not sure I even wanted to go back down. And I was waiting to feel something and it didn't come. Strangely, the only thing I could think about was you."

She blinked in surprise. "Me?"

"Yeah, you." Charlie shook his head. "I hadn't seen you in five years. Hadn't even really thought about you in five years. And then, there you were, clear as day, swimming around in my mind. And here I am." He took a gulp of his wine. "I just want to figure it out."

"So that's all you want with me?"

"No." Charlie grinned as he circled to her side of the table. "I'd really like to kiss you right now. But I'm doing my best to control my impulses."

A satisfied smile curled the corners of her mouth.

"I'm sorry. I shouldn't have jumped to conclusions. I just assumed you were only interested in—" Her gaze met his. "It's nice to see you again, Charlie."

"It's nice being seen." He leaned forward and dropped a kiss on her lips. He'd meant it to be a new beginning, a way to express the sentiment he'd just verbalized. But the moment his mouth touched hers, Charlie felt the ground beneath him shift.

He stared down at her mouth, his breath growing tight in his chest, his thoughts spinning in his head. He wanted to kiss her again, yet he knew it probably wasn't a good idea. But Charlie had operated on sheer instinct for so long that he couldn't stop himself, even if he tried.

He slipped his arm around her waist and gently pulled her body against his, their hips meeting. He found her mouth again only this time, the kiss was far from innocent. He knew exactly what he needed to answer all his questions. And at the moment, that's all he wanted—answers.

Her reaction surprised him. She didn't try to resist, but melted in his embrace, her mouth opening to his tongue and her body arching into his. He had one answer—Evie wanted him as much as he wanted her.

Charlie grabbed her waist and set her on the edge of the worktable, then pulled her thighs against his hips. Though she was four or five inches shorter than he was, this gave him perfect access to her face and mouth, to her neck and shoulders.

"We shouldn't do this," she whispered, twisting away from him and pressing her forehead into his chest. "After you leave, I won't be able to walk into this kitchen without thinking about this."

"I'm not leaving anytime soon," Charlie said.

She looked up at him. "But you will leave," she stated, her voice cool and emotionless.

"We can't stay in this kitchen forever. I'm hoping we'll both leave."

"That's not what I mean," Eve countered with a weak smile.

"Right now, I don't have plans to go anywhere. I'm happy right here."

She sighed softly, then wrapped her arms around his neck. "A week," she said. "That's all I need. Just promise me a week."

But as Charlie kissed her again, he knew that his stay in Boulder would last a lot longer than a week. He needed a new direction in his life and a strange vision on the top of the highest mountain had sent him here.

2

A WEEK WOULD NEVER be enough, Eve thought as she lost herself in the delicious warmth of his mouth. But if he stayed longer, she might be tempted to fall madly in love with him all over again. And if he disappeared too early, she'd be left unsatisfied and longing for more. No, a week would have to suffice.

She smoothed her hands over his chest, remembering how wonderful it felt to touch his skin. He was older now, but his body was still lithe and muscular, everything in such perfect proportion. Wide shoulders, narrow waist, long legs. If they'd been anywhere but her restaurant, she would have stripped the clothes off of him in less than a minute and dragged him to the nearest bed.

But Eve wasn't that same impetuous young woman she'd been five years ago. Back then, she'd believed in love. Now, she was more apt to put her money on lust. There was something to be said for pure physical pleasure, without the expectations that romance brought. And even though she still bore the scars of their last affair, Eve felt confident she could handle whatever he sent her way this time.

She was in a different place in her life now, a place where her career came before everything else, including a relationship with a man. A short-term affair would fit right into her schedule. She had a few weeks before the meetings began with her Seattle investors. And the production team was putting together a final proposal on the television show and wouldn't need her to do a sample episode until next month. Charlie Templeton had shown up at precisely the right time.

When he moved to unbutton her jacket, she impatiently completed the task, tossing it aside and leaving her wearing only a simple camisole beneath. Charlie pressed his mouth into the curve of her neck. Though Eve knew she ought to resist, there wasn't any point. Why pretend she didn't want him? They'd had a past together and the memories of it had rushed back the moment she saw him again.

Her fingers furrowed through his thick hair and Eve tipped her head as his lips drifted lower. But when he reached the last inch of skin above the top of her camisole, Charlie stopped his slow exploration. He stepped back and smiled. "I should probably go," he murmured.

"No!" Eve said. She bit her lip, embarrassed that

she'd reacted so vehemently. "I—I was just going to make myself something to eat. If you're hungry, stay. I'll—feed you."

He stared at her for a long moment, then shrugged. "All right. Just don't make me eat tofu," he warned. "I can't stand that stuff."

Eve slid off the edge of the table, then handed him his glass of wine. "A sandwich," she said, suddenly desperate to keep the evening going. Every instinct told her to beware, but all of that was overwhelmed by the desire that snaked through her bloodstream. "I have some wonderful bread."

As she began to assemble the ingredients on the table, she studied him. When he'd walked into the restaurant that afternoon, Eve had thought she knew exactly what he wanted—sex. But now, she wasn't so sure. The man who used to wait at the front door for her and tear her clothes off the moment she walked inside his house was now taking his own sweet time in seducing her. Had she not made it perfectly clear that she was ready and willing?

"So what's on this sandwich you're making me?"

Eve smiled. "Healthy things."

Charlie growled softly. "You know how I hate healthy things. I like things that are bad for me."

"Is that why you're here?" she asked.

"I told you why I came," Charlie said, reaching out

to snag a cherry tomato from the container. "So, tell me what happened with you and Dan. Or Dave."

"Matt," Eve said. "His name is Matt." Eve carefully sliced a long baguette in half, then smeared it with hummus. "He wasn't the guy I thought I married. It just didn't work out."

"You realized you didn't love him?"

"I realized he didn't love me," she said with a shrug. "And I didn't love him enough to put up with his cheating." She'd seen enough of that with her parents' marriage. She wasn't about to make the same mistakes they'd made, living in a sham of a marriage, pretending to love each other.

"I always thought he was a first-class idiot," Charlie said. "I only saw him that once, but I could tell he didn't know what he had."

"And what did he have?"

"You. He didn't realize he got the best the first time around. But, hey, I could tell he was a real douche from the start."

"Why didn't you warn me?" Eve asked.

"I didn't have a right to interfere," Charlie said.

He watched her silently as she assembled the sandwich, his gaze drifting over her like a lazy caress. She layered on thinly sliced tomatoes and calamata olives, then made a salad of arugula and balsamic dressing and stuffed it in between the two slices of bread. She finished it off with a sprinkling of toasted sunflower seeds, before setting it on a plate in front of him.

The last time they were together, they hadn't had time for cooking. They barely remembered to eat. But things were moving more slowly now and their appetites for other things could be delayed. At least for an hour or two.

Eve waited while he took a big bite of the sandwich. He grinned at her and nodded. "Good," he said as he chewed. "Really good."

She bit into her half of the sandwich. Though she wasn't particularly hungry, eating gave her something to do while looking at Charlie. He was the most beautiful man she'd ever known. Maybe that's why it had been so easy to discount what they'd had together five years ago. She'd just assumed the reason for her attraction to him was because of his physical perfection.

"I could get used to this," he said.

"Eating this late at night really isn't good for you," Eve said. "But it usually takes me a few hours to wind down and I never get a chance to catch a bite when I'm working." She poured a bit more wine into her glass, then refilled his. "Tell me about Everest."

"I don't know if I can. I still haven't figured it all out yet."

"I don't understand."

"It changed me. I went up knowing exactly who

I was and came down a different person. Does that make sense?"

Eve laughed and shook her head. "No." She reached out and wiped a bit of hummus from his lip.

Charlie grabbed her hand and playfully licked it off the end of her finger. But he didn't stop there. He wove his fingers through hers and pulled her hand against his chest.

Their gazes locked and he slowly set his sandwich down to the left of his plate. Eve felt her pulse skip and for a moment, she forgot to breathe. And then, like a wave crashing on the beach, their need for each other overwhelmed them both. This was the way it had been between them five years ago. Nothing had changed.

Their frantic hands tore at each other's clothes as their meal got pushed aside. Charlie pressed her back against the edge of the table, his palms skimming over her body, sliding beneath her shirt to cup her breasts and then moving on to unexplored flesh.

Eve felt dizzy, her knees weak and her mind unable to process what was happening to her. So she let her thoughts drift, focusing only on the sensations racing through her body.

He was gentle, yet determined, as if he knew exactly what they both needed. Eve clutched at the hem of his shirt, gathering it in her fists, holding tight as if it were the only thing keeping him close. She needed this, if only to remind her that she hadn't lost everything in the divorce. She could still want a man, still crave his touch and his taste.

Charlie picked her up and set her back on the table, tugging her camisole over her head and throwing it over his shoulder. Eve glanced down, grateful to see that she'd managed to pick out decent lingerie that day. As he smoothed his hands over her shoulders, she took the opportunity to remove his shirt.

Eve swallowed hard as she took in the sight of him beneath the harsh lights of the kitchen. Though she'd seen his body before, nothing prepared her for the impact that a half-naked man would have on her ability to think—or breathe—or move.

With trembling fingers, she reached out and ran her hand over his smooth chest, his skin warm beneath her touch. It wasn't wrong to want him. She was a grown woman, past the age when she had to worry about denying her sexual needs.

After her divorce, she'd worried that no man would ever want her again, that somehow she'd wasted her one chance at happiness. But Eve was happy now and that was all that mattered.

She waited for him to continue undressing her and when he didn't, she reached for the clasp at the front of her bra. But Charlie caught her fingers and brought them to his lips. "Let's wait with that," he said softly. "We have time."

But his idea of time and hers were two completely

different things. For him, a week was a lifetime and a month, an eternity. He could be with her one moment and halfway around the world the next. Eve closed her eyes, waiting for her heart to stop pounding.

"Evie?" He hooked his finger beneath her chin and tipped her face up. "Look at me." She opened her eyes. "We have time. I promise."

Eve knew promises could easily be broken. But she also sensed Charlie was a man she could trust. Even though he'd left her, he'd never lied to her. "Would you like dessert?"

"Dessert?" He glanced at the remains of their meal. "We haven't finished dinner yet."

Eve slid off the table and walked to the pastry cooler. She pulled out a tofu white-chocolate-and-raspberry mousse that she'd perfected just last week. She found the whipped cream canister on the top shelf and grabbed it. "This is something new. You'll have to tell me what you think."

She added a generous topping of the cream and scooped out a spoonful and held it in front of his lips. He leaned forward and she pulled the spoon away. "Promise you'll tell the truth?"

"I promise."

"I can trust you?"

Charlie paused as he realized that Eve wasn't talking about the dessert. "You can, Evie."

Satisfied, she fed him the mousse and waited for

his reaction. He swallowed, then opened his mouth. "More, please."

"What do you think? Is it good?"

"One more taste."

She scooped out another spoonful and waited. "Well?"

"It's very good," Charlie said. "I like the combination. And it's kind of fluffy so you could eat a lot of it if you wanted to."

"It's made with tofu," she said. "It's a vegan alternative to white chocolate mousse."

"I hate tofu," Charlie said. "But I like this. A lot. So maybe I have changed since the last time we saw each other."

Eve pushed up on her toes and kissed him, then took a spoonful for herself. "It is good. The whipped cream isn't vegan, but I thought it would tempt you."

"Whipped cream always tempts me," he murmured as she scooped out another spoonful for him. He grabbed the canister and sprayed a tiny bit on her bare shoulder, then bent close to lick it off.

"I thought I could add a bit of Amaretto, too. To give it a greater depth of flavor." She sighed softly as his mouth found the spot just below her ear. "What do think of that?"

"I think I'm going to enjoy sharing a meal with you, Evie."

She knew they'd share much more than food over

the next week. But she'd have to be patient and let their meals unfold naturally. Charlie was here with her now and if she just stopped thinking about the future, the present would fall into place.

THEY'D TEASED THEIR way through a late-night dinner at Evie's restaurant, both of them avoiding the logical conclusion to their flirtation. By the time Eve pulled up in front of Charlie's place, he was wondering what had ever possessed him to "take it slow."

"Thanks for the ride," Charlie said, glancing over at Evie, her profile illuminated by the street light. It was almost three in the morning and he didn't want their time together to end. But if he asked her inside, his motives would be painfully obvious. "I probably shouldn't ask you in," he said.

"And I probably shouldn't accept if you did. Are you asking?"

Charlie chuckled. "You know, there are a lot of things in my life I shouldn't have done, but I try not to have any regrets. Would you come in if I asked?"

"Do you have regrets?" Evie asked.

"Yeah. One big one. I shouldn't have left you. I should have stayed a little longer. Just to see."

"See what?" Evie asked.

"I don't know. But I think I might have missed something." He smiled. "Another time. Hey, I was thinking about remodeling my kitchen. I could use your advice. Maybe you could give me some ideas.

I don't know anything about kitchens." He couldn't have come up with a lamer excuse to see her again and he waited for her to shoot him down.

"If it hasn't changed since the last time I was in your house, it could use an update. It's not that late and I'm still wound up from work. Why don't I take a look now?"

Was she really interested in his kitchen, or had she decided to accept his invitation inside? Hell, they both knew what would happen once they stepped over that threshold. Clothes would come off and bodies would come together and they'd both be lost for the next twenty-four to forty-eight hours. "That would be nice," he said.

They got out of the car and slowly strolled up the front walk. "We should probably talk about appliances," he said. "And cabinets. I was thinking about a trash compactor."

"Lots of people think that trash compactors are good for the environment, but they really give you a false sense of accomplishment. Recycling combined with composting would nearly eliminate the need for a trash compactor. We give most of our food waste to a worm farm. They come and pick it up every morning."

Charlie could tell she was nervous. He unlocked the front door and swung it open in front of her. The light from the street filtered inside and she took a few steps forward. Charlie followed her and closed the door, leaving them both in the dark.

He reached out to place his hands on her shoulders and he felt her turn to face him. Evie stepped toward him and a moment later, they were caught in a gentle kiss. Without light, her hesitation seemed to dissolve along with his resolve.

There wasn't much use fighting it. And if he had any doubts about her need for him, they were banished the moment she stripped off his shirt and tossed it aside. Charlie cupped her face in his hands, molding her mouth against his as her hands wandered over his hair. They stumbled backward, kicking off their shoes along the way.

It had been a while since he'd gotten naked with a woman, so his reaction to her touch was immediate and intense. He tugged off her jacket, then drew her camisole over her head. When she brushed up against him, Charlie's breath caught in his throat, the friction causing him to grow even harder.

He steered her toward the leather sofa in the center of the living room. "Tell me you want this," he whispered against her mouth. He didn't want any misunderstandings.

"Yes," she breathed. She grabbed his hand and placed it on her breast, pushing aside the satiny fabric until he touched bare skin. Charlie rubbed his thumb across her nipple, bringing it to a hard peak.

He remembered her body so well and the way

she reacted to his touch had been burned into his brain. Maybe he'd always known he'd come back, that what they'd shared would be revisited one day. That's why he hadn't forgotten her or the way her skin felt beneath his touch.

Spanning her waist with his hands, Charlie pulled her along toward the bedroom, both of them bumping into furniture along the way. But when she cried out, he stopped. Evie bent over at the waist and moaned. "Ow, ow, ow."

"What is it?"

"I stubbed my toe. Ow. Oh, I think it's broken."

Charlie fumbled for the light. When he flipped it on, he found her sitting on the floor, holding her foot, her eyes watering. He squatted down beside her. "Let me see," he said.

She looked up at him, her pretty face etched in a grimace of pain. "No."

He gently pried her fingers away, then lifted her foot to examine it. "Wiggle your toe," he ordered.

She winced, then did as he asked. Gently, he rubbed the hurt away, then drew her foot to his lips and kissed her toe. "Better?"

"No," she said.

He kissed it again. "Now?"

"I think the gods are telling us that we shouldn't do this."

Charlie scooped her up into his arms, then straightened. Compared to the backpack he'd hauled up mountainsides, she was as light as a feather. He nuzzled her neck. "I think the gods have better things to worry about than us," he murmured.

He carried her into the dark bedroom and set her on the bed, then stretched out beside her, pushing her back into the pillows. Furrowing his hands through her hair, he kissed her, taking time to calm her fears. "Better?" he asked.

"Yes," she replied in a breathless voice.

He found the clasp of her bra and unhooked it, then brushed it aside. Her body hadn't changed much in five years, though she'd become a bit curvier. He liked the way she looked, like a woman who occasionally enjoyed a good meal. Charlie had never cared for obsessively thin women or those who used too much makeup or dressed provocatively. In truth, for the past five years, he'd been looking for someone exactly like Eve.

Slowly, they both shed the remainder of their clothes, each item tossed to the floor to make way for a more detailed exploration. Everywhere he touched was perfection, soft and yielding, warm flesh beneath silken skin.

He rolled on top of her, bracing his hands on either side of her body. The heat of his erection pressed against her thighs and she shifted, pulling her legs up along his hips. Charlie held his breath, fighting the urge to slip inside of her.

With a low moan, he trailed a line of kisses from

her shoulder to her breast, taking time to caress her nipple with his tongue. Then he moved lower still, to her belly and then to the damp spot between her legs.

Though they'd done all this before, he hadn't remembered this overwhelming need to please her. This time, he was looking for more than just a physical connection, more than ultimate release. He wanted to possess not just her body, but her heart and her soul.

She was wet already and she guided him to the spot, her fingers tangling in his hair. The moment he touched her with his tongue, she cried out in surprise, her hands clutching, her body twisting.

Charlie waited, then began again, slowly teasing her toward the edge then bringing her back again. He was interested only in her pleasure, in her release. But as he drew her closer, he felt his own need being driven by her response.

She murmured his name, pushing him away. "I want to feel you inside me," she said. Charlie didn't need to be asked twice. He reached for the drawer of the bedside table and retrieved a box of condoms. After tearing a packet open with nervous fingers, he sheathed himself. But he decided to continue what he'd started.

Slowly and deliberately, he caressed her with his tongue and when he was sure she couldn't last any longer, he moved up along her body until he was buried deep within her.

It took only one stroke before she dissolved into her orgasm, her body first arching, and then shuddering in her release. He felt her spasms and a moment later, Charlie joined her, waves of pleasure washing over him until he was lost in the intensity of their coupling.

They rode the crest for what seemed like forever. And when they were both completely spent, Charlie rolled off of her, pulling her body against his. She pressed a kiss to the center of his chest and he inhaled the sweet scent of her hair.

"How is your toe?" he asked.

"What toe?" she murmured, with a soft giggle.

"Hmm. I think we've come up with a cure for stubbed toes." He drew back and looked down into her face, filling in the details that the dark room did not allow. "So what are we going to do about this? Because I want to spend a lot more time with you."

"Naked?" she asked.

"Yes. But clothed, too."

"How long are you going to stay this time?"

"I don't know," he said.

"A week?"

"At least," Charlie said. Was that all she wanted of him? Just a week? It didn't seem like enough time. But he could give her at least that. And maybe, after a week, she'd want another and another.

"Right now, I think I could stay here for a year. Maybe ten or twenty."

She brushed her lips against his. "Don't make any promises you can't keep," she whispered.

Maybe it was time he started making promises, Charlie mused. If he wanted someone to share his life, then he had to be willing to give something in return. And no matter how he looked at it, Eve belonged in his life. Now he'd just have to convince her.

EVE OPENED HER EYES, rubbing the sleep from them as she peered at her surroundings. This wasn't her bedroom. It took a moment for her to remember where she was—Charlie's house. They'd spent the night together and sometime in the hours before dawn, she'd fallen asleep.

She rolled over to find Charlie's half of the bed cold and empty. The scent of bacon and coffee hung in the air and she could hear noise coming from the kitchen. Eve grabbed his shirt from the floor and pulled it over her naked body, then got to her feet.

She found him standing in front of the stove, dressed in a faded pair of jeans and nothing more. "What are you doing?" she asked before stifling a yawn.

"Making breakfast," Charlie said, glancing over his shoulder. "Are you hungry?"

She stood next to him and stared at the bacon

draining on top of a paper towel. "Not for that. Do you know what's in bacon? You might as well just swallow a handful of deadly chemicals."

"I love bacon," Charlie said. "Everything tastes better with bacon." An English muffin popped out of the toaster. He slathered it with butter and honey and offered it to her. "No chemicals in this. All natural, whole grain."

She reluctantly took a bite. "Well, Bacon Boy, I'm proud of you. Are the eggs in that omelet from free-range chickens?"

"I don't know. The chickens weren't hanging out at the store so I didn't have a chance to ask. Are you really going to be that fussy and ruin my efforts here?"

Eve sighed, realizing there was a proper time to stand on her soapbox and a time to kick it aside. "Sorry. But when I'm doing the cooking, I'm going to make sure you eat healthy."

"Does that mean that when I'm doing the cooking, you'll eat unhealthy?" he asked, waving a piece of bacon in front of her face. "Tempted?"

"It takes a lot more than bacon to tempt me," she said before taking another bite of the muffin.

Charlie grabbed her hand and took a bite of the muffin, then grinned. "You were tempted last night."

She felt a blush warm her cheeks. "That was different. What you were offering was...healthy...and natural. Low in cholesterol and calories, and high on fun. If bacon had as much to offer, maybe I'd start sleeping with a slab under my pillow."

"I'm not sure I could give up meat," he said, taking a bite of the bacon. "I'm a guy. We need protein or we can't function. And don't tell me I can get protein from tofu or those sprouty things."

"You should at least stick to fish. And chicken, maybe."

He flipped the omelet he was cooking, then cut it in half and slid the pieces onto two plates. "Veggies and cheese inside."

"When did you learn to cook?" she asked as she grabbed a fork.

"I've always known how to cook. My mom worked full-time after my dad died. Me and my sister and brother were left to take care of ourselves. Lena did the cleaning, Ben took care of the yard and I cooked." He handed her a pepper grinder. "As I recall, the last time we were together, we didn't think a whole lot about food."

"We're more mature now," she teased. "We have our priorities in order." She took a bite of her omelet. "You never told me much about your family." In fact, she'd never asked. Their first relationship had been all about sex. She'd always thought they'd have time to get to know each other. "How old were you when your dad died?"

"Ten," he said. "He was a good man. He worked

really hard and we didn't see much of him. He traveled a lot on business."

"Is that why you're always chasing bigger and better adventures?"

"What do you mean?"

"Were you running from your own mortality?"

"I don't know," he said, as if taken aback by the notion. "Maybe. Someone else told me the same thing."

"Men do that," she said. "That's why they cheat on their wives. To make themselves feel young and virile. Climbing a mountain will do the same thing. You get addicted to the thrill." She sighed softly, then turned her attention back to her omelet.

"I gotta tell you, last night was pretty thrilling."

Eve looked up to see him staring at her. A shiver skittered through her as she remembered all that had passed between them. "For me, too. It's... It's been a while. Really, a long while. Too long."

"For me, too."

"Two years?" she asked.

He drew in a deep breath, then shook his head. "Not quite that long."

"So you thought I'd be a sure thing?" she asked.

"No," he said, his tone adamant.

"What did you have planned when you stopped by the restaurant?"

"A drink and some conversation. But it seems like we always get distracted when we're together."

"I'm not surprised we ended up in bed," she said. "We never really had an end to things five years ago."

"We didn't? I thought you marrying Dave put a nice tidy period at the end of it."

"I married Dave because—"

"Matt," he corrected.

"I know!" Eve cried. "I just thought it was easier to go along. Which is exactly what I did with Matt. He seemed like the easy choice," she said. "The path of least resistance. You would have been the difficult choice. Besides, you just disappeared in the middle of the night. I didn't have to choose. You did that for me."

"Well, I won't be doing that again," Charlie said. He stepped around the counter and grabbed her by the waist, pulling her into a long, deep kiss. "I'm sticking around for a while." He tugged her toward the hall. "Come on, I want you back in my bed. We need to work up an appetite for lunch."

"I have to be at the restaurant in an hour," she protested. But her resistance was weak at best. She had a staff of kitchen help who knew exactly what to do to prepare for the lunch crowd. And Lily would be there to supervise. She deserved a day off every now and then.

He wrapped his arms around her thighs and picked her up. "I'll have you there in forty-five minutes," he teased. "Or six hours. Depending upon how good I am."

There was no doubt about his skills in the bedroom, she mused. And six hours sounded like just about the right amount of time to satisfy all her cravings. They'd enjoy a sexual feast now and she'd deal with the famine later.

3

HE HEARD THE KEY IN THE LOCK and Charlie smiled. He and Evie had spent the last three nights together and this would make a fourth. Though their nights began late, usually around midnight, they could afford to sleep in. Eve usually left for the restaurant at eleven.

"I'm in here," he called when he heard her footsteps heading toward the kitchen. A few moments later, she appeared at the end of the sofa, a bag slung over her shoulder. "What's that?" he asked, pointing to the bag.

"I'm tired of rushing home to shower and grab fresh clothes in the morning. So I brought a few things along. If you have a problem with that, then tough."

Charlie grinned. "No problem. But we should probably set some ground rules if you're planning to move in."

"I'm not moving in. I'm just visiting. Both you and I know that this is a short-term thing."

"You could move in," he said. "It would make things more convenient." There was a time in his life when he never would have made a suggestion like that, but now, the prospect of having Evie with him full-time had distinct advantages.

"No. I think we're fine the way things are." She dropped her bag on the floor, then sat down next to him on the sofa. "What are you doing?"

"Putting together a slide presentation on the seven summits. I'm doing a couple of lectures at the university next week."

"So that's why you came back," she said. "It wasn't for me."

"No. Not technically. But when I accepted the job, I knew I might see you again."

"Show me," Evie said, pointing to the computer. "I'd like to see what took you away from me the first time."

Over the next two hours, Charlie went through the photos he'd compiled, explaining the challenges of each climb and the significance in his quest. They opened a bottle of wine and curled up together, the computer resting on his lap and Evie tucked beneath his arm.

When it was over, she took a deep breath and sighed. "I don't understand it," she said. "You risk your life. People die. They freeze to death or fall. For what?"

"I don't know," he said.

"What do you mean, you don't know?"

"I used to believe that it was about the challenge, facing nature head-on and coming out the winner. Conquering my environment. You do it, too. I've seen you in the kitchen. When things seem to be the most chaotic, you get this look on your face. This determination to overcome anything that fate throws in your way."

"No," she said. "There's no comparison. My life doesn't hang in the balance because of a cheese soufflé. Weren't you scared you might die out there?"

"No," he said. "I never thought about it."

"Maybe that's because you didn't have something to live for," she said.

"Maybe," he murmured.

She was right. If he'd had a wife and kids, he wouldn't have had the nerve to risk his life. Even now, after just a few days with Evie, the stakes were suddenly so much higher. Though he didn't have her—not yet—there was the possibility he might have her sometime. And that was enough to keep him on level ground.

"And it's not all that dangerous," he said. "It is if you make stupid decisions. But if you're smart, the odds are pretty good you'll get up and down safely."

"So, what's next?" she asked.

"I thought maybe you'd like a bath," Charlie replied. "You always take a shower before bed. I thought a bath might be nice."

"I meant, where are you going next?"

"I know what you meant. I don't know. I'm just thinking about a bath right now."

"You just want me to take my clothes off," she said.

"I could take them off for you if you don't want to," he suggested.

"Go ahead," she murmured. "I'm too tired to move."

He pulled her to her feet and led her to the bathroom. As he filled the tub, Charlie slowly undressed her. He loved the way her body moved beneath his touch, always seeking the warmth of his hands. He'd become incredibly possessive over the past few days, almost jealous of the time she'd spent with her ex.

As he skimmed her jeans down over her hips, she wrapped her arms around his neck and closed her eyes. He took his time as he came back up, smoothing his palms over her hips and torso. Though he'd grown familiar with her curves, her body never failed to intrigue him.

He wanted to know about the tiny scar on her knee and why she always painted her toes red but left her fingernails untouched. He wanted to analyze the patterns of freckles on her arms and memorize the scent of her hair. Would these things ever begin to bore him? Or would he always find things to intrigue him?

When she was completely naked, he helped her into the tub, then sat on the floor beside it. "This is wonderful," she murmured, sinking into the hot water. "I never take baths."

"Maybe you should start," he said, smoothing his hand over her damp shoulder.

"It's relaxing," she said, her eyes closing and her lips parting slightly.

He watched her as she drifted off to sleep, her body relaxing completely and her features growing soft and girlish. Charlie couldn't remember ever feeling this content. He wasn't thinking about where he had to be next or what he had to do to get there. He wanted to be here with Eve, to fall asleep with her in his arms and to wake up to the sight of her pretty face.

"God, you're really losing it," he murmured, smoothing a strand of hair out of her eyes. This was crazy. Something had happened to him on that mountaintop. The lack of oxygen had scrambled his brain. He was actually imagining he'd fallen in love with Eve.

He stared at her face, at the features that had quickly become so familiar to him. Something was driving him forward, pushing him to learn more, to deepen their relationship just to see where it took them both.

Maybe this was just another adventure, he mused, another environment to conquer. But what then? Would he move on? Would she turn into just another conquest? God, he didn't want to hurt her. Though she wouldn't admit it, his leaving five years ago had changed the course of her life—and not necessarily for the better.

He was determined not to make a mess of this a second time. When and if he left, it would be her decision, not his. For now, he'd stay as long she wanted him.

"Evie?" Charlie smoothed a palm over her cheek. "Sweetheart, wake up."

She opened her eyes and smiled. "Did I fall asleep?"

Charlie nodded. Hell, what did he expect? She hadn't had more than four or five hours' sleep the past three nights and she'd put in a full day of work after each. Maybe it was time to spend the night sleeping. "Come on, let's put you to bed." He helped her out of the tub then grabbed a towel from the basket and wrapped it around her. She followed him to the bedroom, stumbling over her own feet along the way.

When he pulled back the covers, she crawled beneath them and moaned softly. Charlie quickly stripped off his clothes and lay down behind her, tucking her body into the curve of his.

He expected her to drift off, but instead she moved against him until he was fully aroused. They didn't speak, but it was clear what she wanted. And when he sheathed himself and gently pushed inside her, she moaned softly. It wasn't like their previous encounters in the bedroom—wild and passionate, desperate.

This was gentle, almost soothing. For a long time, he barely moved, enjoying the warmth that surrounded him. To Charlie's surprise, he found himself dancing perilously close to the edge, the power of his release relegated to his mind rather than his body.

Reaching around, he touched her, slipping his fingers between her folds and caressing that spot that made her crazy with need. She arched back against him, resting her hand on his hip. And when the spasms rocked her body, it was more than enough to send him over the edge.

They didn't say a word to each other, yet Charlie was aware of a silent pact that they'd made with each other. Her body was his refuge, a secret place he'd found that no one else could share, a place where he could lay his soul bare without fears or doubts.

Evie had given him that gift and with it came a grave responsibility. Her happiness had become inextricably intertwined with his. They were no longer two separate people. They had a relationship now, a bond that couldn't easily be broken.

He closed his eyes and nuzzled his face into the hair at her nape. Was he feeling the first stirrings of love? Or was he merely trying to convince himself that he was capable of experiencing that emotion?

In the end, it didn't matter. Everything would become much clearer with time. And Charlie had more than enough time to invest in the woman lying next to him.

"YOU NEED DECENT FOOTWEAR," he said, staring into the window of the outdoor equipment store. "If we're going to do any hiking, you have to have boots. Come on, let's go inside and get you a pair."

Charlie grabbed Eve's hand and she reluctantly followed him inside. He'd become particularly obsessed with taking her hiking and Eve had to wonder what was behind the obsession. She had been quite content to spend the previous week in bed, but Charlie seemed to be growing less interested in marathon sex and more interested in…exercise.

Eve wondered if this was just a prelude to the inevitable, a way to ease her into the notion of him leaving again. Though his first lecture at the university was scheduled for the end of the week, and the second four days later, it was conceivable he could pack his bags and leave the moment he was finished.

Eve had to prepare herself for that eventuality. And though she'd done her best to maintain an indifferent attitude about the future, she knew their parting would come with at least a small amount of pain.

She'd grown used to having him near, to coming

home to him each night, to exhausting herself in his arms before she fell asleep. It would be so simple to fall in love with Charlie Templeton, if she'd only allow herself that luxury. But Eve had learned a few things from her failed marriage, the most important being never to depend upon a man for her happiness.

Charlie picked up a hiking boot from a display and handed it to her. "These are the best," he said. "I have a pair. They're easy to break in and they're waterproof."

"Why would they have to be waterproof? We're not going hiking if it rains."

"We may have to walk through streams," he said. "And if your feet get damp, they get cold and you get blisters. Believe me, dry feet are important."

"These boots weigh a ton," she said.

"They're sturdy. You can't hike in Birkenstocks," he said. "Or those silly plastic clogs you wear in the kitchen."

"Why do we have to hike at all? There are perfectly decent sidewalks all over Boulder. We could just…stroll," Eve said.

"Nope. We're going to get some real exercise. You're feeding me far too much and I have to work it off. Since I want to spend as much time as possible with you, I figure you can come along and get some exercise, too."

"I hate exercise," Eve said.

"For someone who is so conscious about what you eat, you don't do a very good job with the rest of the equation." He turned to the salesperson, a petite college student with a nose ring. "We'd like to see these in a size…"

"Seven," Eve said.

"Bring us a seven and a half, too," Charlie added. "You should wear heavy socks with them."

Eve sat down on a nearby bench and kicked off her Birkenstocks. "You know, I eat well because I hate to exercise. I've had to make compromises."

Charlie sat down next to her, wrapped his arm around her neck and kissed the top of her head. "You'll like it. I promise. I'll make it fun. We'll go camping. And you can cook over an open fire. Won't that be a challenge?"

Eve had been so busy at work the past weekend, she and Charlie hadn't had much time together beyond their time in bed. But carving out hours in the day for recreation seemed a bit strange—and a waste of what little time they had left. But she'd given him a peek into her world at the restaurant. Maybe he was interested in doing the same. His world was the great outdoors.

Since the moment she'd set eyes on him again, Eve felt as though the connection they'd made five years ago had survived their time apart. Everything felt comfortable and easy with Charlie. And there was no denying the sex was good.

But she'd fooled herself once before with Matt, imagining that everything was perfect between them, only to discover that she'd been wrong all along. She'd have to try harder to maintain her objectivity with Charlie, especially when he was doing everything in his power to charm her.

"I thought we could leave tomorrow afternoon," he said.

"Leave?"

"We'll drive up into the mountains. I know a beautiful spot to camp, right by a lakeshore. It's about a two-hour hike in. We'll spend the night and then hike back out in the morning."

"I have to work," Eve said.

"Come on," he replied. "You know as well as I do that the restaurant can do without you for a night. It's a Tuesday. No one eats out on a Tuesday." He leaned closer. "Have you ever had sex in the great outdoors?"

"No," she said. "Have you?"

"No," he said.

"You are such a liar."

"Eve, when I'm with you, everything feels like the first time."

There wasn't much she could say to that, Eve mused. She knew exactly how he felt. When they were together, her past experiences with men seemed to fade away until her only memories were of Charlie. "Good answer," she said.

The salesperson handed Charlie two shoeboxes and he removed the larger pair and strung the laces through the hooks and eyes. Then he retrieved a pair of wool socks from a nearby rack and slipped them on her bare feet.

Eve watched as he tucked her foot inside the right boot and laced it up. This was his world, she mused. She was comfortable with knives and graters and small electric appliances, the smells and sounds of the kitchen. Charlie lived in a different world, a world of skies and streams, fresh air and rocky ground.

"How do they feel?" he asked after he'd laced up the second boot.

"Like I'm wearing cement overshoes," Eve replied, rising to her feet. "And they're so attractive."

He looked up at her and gave her an impatient glare. "You'll get used to them. Just wear them for the rest of the day to break them in."

Eve glanced at her watch. She and Charlie had shared a late lunch together, eating at one of Eve's favorite Chinese restaurants a few blocks from the Garden Gate. "I need to get back," she said. "My sous-chef took the day off and I've got a lot of prep to do for this week. Especially if I'm taking tomorrow off."

He handed the sales clerk his credit card and Eve reached for it. "You don't have to pay for these," she said.

"I want to. I'm pretty sure you wouldn't be buying

them yourself, so they'll be my treat. And just to make sure you wear them today, I'm keeping your Birkenstocks." He put her shoes in the empty box, then leaned over and kissed her softly. "I'll see you later tonight."

"Why don't you come in for a late supper?" she suggested.

"I'll do that," he said. "I'll see you later."

Eve hurried out of the store, nearly tripping over herself in the hiking boots. Though she knew she looked foolish in them, the residents of Boulder were quite forgiving when it came to outlandish outfits. Boulder was a city of wildly diverse individuals. On her way back to the restaurant she saw plenty of tie-dyed T-shirts, Western wear and bicycle shorts.

The dining room was empty when she walked in the front door. She smiled at Sarah, who was stacking glasses behind the bar, then strolled into the kitchen. Lily had the luncheon receipts spread across the worktable.

"There you are!" she said, spinning around to face Eve. Her gaze took in the boots and she frowned. "What are those on your feet?"

"Hiking boots," Eve said. "Charlie bought them for me."

"What happened to lingerie or perfume or a nice bouquet of roses?"

"He said I'd need them if we go hiking," Eve explained.

"And you'd need a parachute if you were going to jump out of a plane. But I can't see you doing either of those things."

"I can be outdoorsy," Eve said. "Besides, hiking is just walking...uphill...over rocks and branches and stuff. How hard can it be?"

"You must really love this guy," Lily said.

"No!" Eve cried. "Far from it. I'm trying my best not to love him."

"Be careful," Lily murmured. "I know how long it took you to get over Matt."

"This is different. I'm not planning to marry Charlie."

The kitchen door swung open and Sarah poked her head inside. "Eve, you have a visitor."

"Oh, good grief," Lily said. "Can't he spend a minute away from you?"

"It's not Charlie," Sarah said. "It's your ex-husband."

Eve glanced up at Lily and winced. "What does he want?"

"He didn't say. He looks a little...nervous?"

Eve nodded. "I can't imagine why he's here, unless he's looking for a free lunch." She pointed at Lily. "You stay in the kitchen. I don't need you stirring things up with him."

Lily had never been fond of Matt and she wasn't shy about letting her hatred show. They'd met while Eve was going through her divorce. When it had come time to buy Matt out of the restaurant, Lily had decided to come in as a partner. It had been the best thing to ever happen to the Garden Gate. Lily was a wonderful business manager and a good friend.

When Eve emerged from the kitchen, she found Matt sitting at the bar, a half-empty glass of beer in front of him. She stood at the door watching him, wondering what she'd ever seen in him. He was self-involved and immature and a…a wimp. "Matt," she murmured, as she stepped up beside him. "What can I do for you?"

He turned and smiled, but Eve could see it was forced. "Eve. Hi. Wow, you look good. How long has it been?"

"A while," she said. "Why are you here?"

It was clear he'd expected some polite chitchat before getting down to the business at hand, but Eve didn't have time to stroke his ego and make him feel comfortable. "Word around town is that you've got a new boyfriend. People have seen you out together."

"So? I'm single. I'm allowed to date. You dated while we were married and it didn't seem to bother you then." She sighed. "What do you want?"

"I also heard you've been talking to some investors about a restaurant in Seattle."

"Where did you hear that?" Eve asked.

"A reliable source."

"What do you want, Matt?"

He looked uneasy and a bit pale. "Business has

been a little down lately. And I—I figure since I helped build your business, I should get a share of anything that comes out of it like this new restaurant. Of course, if you want to buy me out right away, we could negotiate a fair price."

"Buy you out of what?" Eve said, staring at him in astonishment. He really was an idiot. How could she have missed that?

Matt cleared his throat. "A lawyer friend of mine mentioned that I might want to consider renegotiating the divorce settlement, seeing as how it's had such a negative impact on my earning ability."

"Did you ever think maybe it was your bad behavior that had an effect on your business? Messing around with college-age girls doesn't make you look particularly responsible."

"Come on, Eve. Both you and I know that our marriage was a mistake from the beginning. You didn't want me anymore than I wanted you."

"Get out of here," she said. "If you want to try to renegotiate the settlement, feel free. But I don't think there's a judge in this county who will side with you."

Eve could see that he hadn't expected the response she gave. In the past, Eve might just have given him the money, hoping to keep their relationship pleasant. But she wanted Matt out of her life. If she paid him, he'd be back for more.

"I'm not looking for much," Matt said. "I just have

some…unexpected expenses. My lawyer says I've got a good case."

"Great. Go for it. Show the entire city of Boulder what a horrible excuse for a husband you were."

He stood up and drained the rest of his beer, then set it down on the bar. "You don't have to be so nasty."

It felt liberating to tell him off, Eve mused. She was slamming the door shut on that part of her life and moving on. "I made a mistake five years ago," Eve said. "But I'm not going to make another one tonight. If you come after me for more money, I will spend every last cent I have making sure you don't get anything. Now get out of my restaurant."

He walked to the door, his shoulders slumped. When he was finally outside, Eve leaned back against the bar and tried to slow her pounding pulse. She'd never loved him, that much was clear to her now. And he'd never loved her. Their marriage *had* been a huge mistake.

"Good for you."

Eve looked over to find Lily watching her from the kitchen door. She smiled weakly at her friend. "Thanks. It felt good. How could I have been so stupid? Why couldn't I see what kind of man he was?"

"Maybe you were in love with someone else?" Lily offered.

"Maybe," Eve admitted.

Perhaps Charlie had been the reason her marriage had failed. Maybe, deep down in the secret corners of her heart, she'd loved him and not Matt. And now they had a second chance to make things right.

But did she have the courage to put her heart on the line all over again? Or would she let another chance pass her by?

"THIS IS WEIRD," CHARLIE said, glancing over his shoulder at Jack's two kids sitting silently in the backseat of the SUV. "I haven't spent a whole lot of time around kids." He lowered his voice. "They're kind of scary."

"Yeah, just don't look them in the eye or they'll throw themselves on the ground and pitch a fit."

"Don't they talk?"

"Sure," Jack said. "But if they're quiet in the car, we stop for ice cream. I have them trained well. Their mother doesn't like them to have sweets." Jack looked in the rearview mirror. "You guys can talk. You're starting to scare Charlie a little bit."

The boy and girl both grinned then launched into a series of unrelated questions. Was his watch waterproof? Did he own a dog? How many pieces of bubblegum could he fit in his mouth at once? Was he going to get ice cream, too?

They were odd kids. The boy was nearly nine and the girl had just turned six. According to Jack, they were both quite bright and inquisitive, but easily bored and distracted. Though they were on their best behavior at the moment, Jack had warned Charlie that they could have a meltdown at any moment, for any reason.

Charlie tried to answer their questions, one by one, and the conversation slowly disintegrated into silliness, with a long series of poop and fart jokes. Jack seemed completely oblivious to it all. Charlie was almost relieved when they pulled up to the park. The kids jumped out of the car and ran toward the playground equipment, while Jack grabbed the basketball from the cargo area.

"Aren't you worried about them?" Charlie asked. "How are we going to play ball and watch them at the same time?"

"Don't worry," Jack said. "As a parent, you develop a very keen sense of where they are at all times. It's like they have a built-in global positioning chip. If they wander too far, an alarm goes off in your head. And then there's always their instinct to tattle on each other. If one does something wrong, the other will scream bloody murder in a matter of seconds. They monitor each other's behavior."

Charlie shook his head. "I don't know how you do it. It's got to be overwhelming. You're responsible for making sure they don't both turn into a couple of losers."

"You just do your best," Jack said. "They're good kids. Most of the time. Hell, look at you. You didn't have a dad for most of your teenage years and you turned out all right." Jack dribbled the ball, then took a jump shot. "Do you want to play some one-on-one or should we play HORSE?"

"I think we should stick to HORSE," Charlie said. "I haven't played basketball in a couple years. There aren't a whole lot of courts at base camp."

Jack tossed him the ball. "You start. For every one you miss, you get a letter and you have to answer a question."

"A question about what?"

"It can be about anything. But you have to be completely honest."

Charlie smiled as he remembered. It was the same way they'd played it when they were in college. It was so much easier to talk about sticky subjects when they had basketball to focus on. "All right." He took a shot from the baseline and missed.

"How is it going with the girl? Eve, is that her name?" Jack asked.

"It's going well. Really well. We spend every night together. The sex is incredible. She's funny and smart and she's an incredible cook, even though all she cooks is vegetables. I'm taking her camping tomorrow, so she might even like the outdoors."

Jack took a shot from the top of the key and missed. Charlie scooped up the rebound and dribbled over to the right corner. "Your turn," he said. "Were you there when your kids were born? I mean, did you see it all?"

"Sure," Jack said. "It was pretty cool. I got to hold them right away and cut the cord. They were all slimy and red. They looked like hell. But they got a lot cuter after a few months. And once they started walking and talking, the fun began." Jack chuckled. "You wouldn't believe half the stuff that comes out of their mouths."

Charlie took his shot and made it. Jack jogged over and took the same shot and missed. "That's H," Charlie said. "So is it true what they say? That your sex life goes to hell after you have kids?"

"Things change," Jack said. "But it stops being about the sex. That's not really how we express our feelings for each other. At least, not exclusively. It's about making a home and watching over each other. Helping each other through the rough times. Cleaning up the puke, taking out the garbage, snaking the drain in the kitchen sink. Those are the kind of things that Jenny loves. When I do those things, the sex gets even better."

"When did you know you were in love with her?" Charlie asked.

"Man, you have it bad, don't you?" Jack said. "I can hear it in your voice."

"No," Charlie said. "I'm just curious, that's all."

"When did I know I was in love with Jenny? We were playing softball. You were there, remember?

She took a line drive to the face and went down. She was crying and her makeup was running down her face and her nose had swollen up to twice its size. She asked me if it looked bad and I couldn't bring myself to tell her the truth. I told her she looked beautiful. And it was the truth. At that moment, she was the most beautiful woman in the world to me. She still is. That's when I realized I had to marry her."

"I get that," Charlie said. "I used to be into a woman's looks. The hair, the boobs, the butt. It made a difference in the attraction I felt. But with Eve, I don't really think about those things. She's just...Eve. And she's perfect exactly the way she is. In fact, I really like the imperfections."

"So what are you going to do about this girl?" Jack asked.

"I don't know. I guess I'm going to have to see where it all goes and then I'll decide."

"Don't let her get away," Jack warned. "It's the worst thing you can do. If she's the one and you mess it up, Charlie, you're going to regret it for the rest of your life." He chuckled. "And just think, a few years from now you can have a couple of those." He pointed to his kids. "Brenna, don't eat sand. Garrett, why would you let her do that? Come over here, both of you."

Charlie watched as Jack tended to his children, wiping his daughter's face clean with the hem of his T-shirt and gently scolding his son. In all the years

Charlie had known Jack, he'd never once imagined him in the role of father. But Jack was good at it. He seemed to maintain a sense of humor, even when his children misbehaved. And it was apparent that his children adored him.

"You know what would get rid of that nasty taste in your mouth, Brenna? Ice cream. I think we should go get some right now. In fact, I know a place where we can find the best ice cream sundaes in town." Charlie reached out and took the little girl's hand. "I know the lady who makes them."

"Where are we going?" Brenna asked.

"A place not too far from here," Charlie said. "The owner will make us whatever we want." He glanced over at Jack. "I might as well introduce you."

"This is a first," Jack said.

"You'll like her," Charlie said. "And whatever you do, tell her you like her boots."

They drove downtown and parked a half block from the restaurant. The dining room had a scattering of guests and Charlie saw Eve sitting at the end of the bar, a bottle of wine open in front of her and a man he didn't recognize.

The guy wasn't any older than Eve and was dressed in casual business attire, a freshly pressed shirt and trousers and a navy blazer. Charlie glanced down at his clothes, a T-shirt and a pair of cargo shorts. He thought about running home to change, but his curiosity got the better of him.

The bartender recognized him and gave him a wave, then leaned over to Eve and informed her of his arrival. She turned and smiled, then slid off the bar stool to greet him. "Hi," she said. "What are you doing here?"

"I promised these two an ice cream sundae," he said, pointing to Garrett and Brenna. "Can you fix us up?"

"Sure," she said.

"Hi," Jack said, holding out his hand. "They belong to me. I'm Jack Finnegan and this is Garrett and Brenna. I'm an old friend of Charlie's."

"This is Eve," Charlie said. "Eve Keller. Jack is my college roommate."

"It's nice to meet you," she said. "You're the first friend of Charlie's I've met."

"I could say the same for you," Jack replied. "Charlie's been telling me all about you."

Her eyebrow went up and she glanced back and forth between the two of them. "Really?"

"About your cooking," Jack said. "And...other things."

"Well, why don't I take the kids back into the kitchen and we'll get started on the sundaes? You guys look like you could use something to drink. Kenny, get these boys a cold beer, would you? And finish up the wine order with Ed."

Charlie watched as she escorted the kids through

the bar and into the kitchen. Unlike him, she didn't seem to be nervous around children.

"She's nice," Jack said.

"She is. And beautiful. And smart. And talented." He looked over at Jack. "And I'd be a fool to let her go, wouldn't I?"

"Yeah, you would. She runs a restaurant. You could have all the free food and beer you wanted. I should bring Jenny here for dinner. She'd like this place."

"They only serve vegetables," Charlie murmured, watching Eve through the open door of the kitchen.

"Jenny is crazy about salad. That's all she ever eats. You two should come over for a barbeque some night this week."

"Only if you barbeque vegetables," Charlie said. "That's all Eve eats.

"I can do that," Jack said.

Charlie smiled. This was a big step, finding mutual friends, socializing with other couples. It's what normal people did when they were involved in a relationship. And wasn't that what Charlie had been looking to experience—a normal relationship?

"I'll bring the beer," Charlie said.

4

"DO WE HAVE TO DO THIS NOW?" Eve asked. She dipped her spoon into the pint of ice cream she was eating and took a bite, savoring the creamy taste. After the sundaes that afternoon, Charlie had insisted she bring home a variety of the homemade ice creams she served in the restaurant. He'd finished the chocolate truffle after dinner and she was working on the butter pecan. "Thinking about redesigning your kitchen is too much like work."

They'd spent the past four hours in bed and it was now nearly three in the morning. Eve sat on the counter next to the sink in Charlie's kitchen and Charlie was sprawled in a kitchen chair dressed only in his boxer shorts, eating a bowl of cereal. "I was just thinking since you like to cook so much, I'd make this kitchen a bit nicer."

"Oh," she said, feigning shock. "It's not enough

that you use me for sex. Now you want me to cook for you as well?"

Though her words were meant to tease, she felt a certain sense of pride that she could satisfy both his stomach and his libido. Men were so simple. Sex and food. That's all they really required to be happy.

"No!" Charlie said. "I just want you to be comfortable here. And I know decent appliances are what you're used to." He stood up and crossed to where she was perched, setting his bowl in the sink. "I have a surprise for you." He pulled the drawer open next to her legs and withdrew a kitchen knife, still resting in its store package.

Eve stared at it for a moment. First, the hiking boots and now this. It was an odd gift, but she knew the brand and the price tag that came along with it. "You bought this for me?"

"Yeah. It's kind of like keeping your toothbrush in my bathroom. Now you have a knife you can keep in my kitchen."

"These knives are expensive," she said, taking the package from his hand. Her gaze met his and she smiled. "Thank you."

"You're welcome," he said, dropping a kiss on her lips. Charlie stepped between her legs and slid his palms up along her thighs, letting them come to rest on her hips. She was naked beneath his t-shirt and though they'd just spent hours in bed, his touch still had the capacity to send a thrill racing through her body.

"Are you going to share that ice cream or are you going to eat it all yourself?" he asked.

She held out a spoonful of the butter pecan and then fed it to him.

"So what do you think?" he continued. "What should I do with this kitchen? Should I tear everything out and start from scratch?"

"No," she said, shaking her head. "The cabinets are gorgeous. They're original to the house. The leaded glass in them would cost a fortune to reproduce. I'd have them stripped and refinished. And then maybe hire a cabinet maker to replicate them so that you could put a few more on that wall." She pointed to the spot beneath her. "Take this one out and put in a dishwasher."

"What else?" he asked.

Eve sighed. He seemed to be obsessed with his kitchen. This was the third time he'd brought it up today—once at the restaurant after Jack and his family had left, once more when they were making dinner and now again. "The sink and countertops need to be replaced. There's probably a hardwood floor under the linoleum. If it's in good shape, you could strip it. I'd put granite in for the countertops. Although concrete might look really cool. Then you need to upgrade the appliances."

"After all that, would this be a kitchen you could cook in?" he asked.

She frowned. "Sure."

"Good," he said. "I'll get started on it next week."

"Why? Hire someone to do it after you leave," she suggested. "Then you don't have to put up with the mess."

"I'm not planning on going anywhere, so there's no reason not to start now," he said.

Eve stifled a gasp. Though they hadn't talked about the future, she'd just assumed that he'd be off on another adventure within the month. Actually, she was counting on it. Too much time with Charlie Templeton was not a good thing. "What do you mean?" she asked, the spoon frozen halfway to her mouth.

"I'm going to stick around for a while."

"How long is 'a while'?"

"I don't know," Charlie said. "Longer than a few weeks. Longer than a month. Maybe even longer than a year."

"When did you decide this?" she asked. "And why didn't you tell me?"

"What difference does it make?"

She slid off the counter and shoved the ice cream into his hands. "It makes a lot of difference. I thought you were going to leave like you did last time. That's what I was prepared for."

"You want me to leave?"

"Yes!" She cursed softly. "No. I just—" Eve drew a deep breath. "I want to be prepared."

"For what? I don't understand."

"This is supposed to be a short affair and nothing more. After a week or two, it will end and we'll both get on with our lives. That's all I want. That's all I can handle right now."

He stared at her in utter confusion, his brow knit into a frown and his eyes filled with suspicion. "So you want me to leave? What if I don't?"

Eve stiffened her spine at the challenge in his voice. "You're free to do whatever you want. I'm just saying that what's happening between us won't necessarily continue."

"Fine," he said. "But now I feel like I'm the one being used."

"I just think it would be better if we kept things simple between us."

"Right." He shrugged. "I'm cool with that. Simple is better."

Eve could hear the anger in his voice. They'd never argued before, though she knew Charlie could be stubborn when he didn't get his own way. Though they'd only been together for a short time, already this was beginning to feel like a real relationship. And though Eve wanted to believe that there might be a future for them, she couldn't indulge in a fantasy that might never come true.

Charlie was a drifter, unable to settle down in one place, unable to commit to one woman. She knew it and so did he. And this silly attempt to pretend differently was a delusion that would hurt them both. He'd been spending time with his friend Jack and no doubt had developed a case of envy.

"Don't be angry. I'm just not that anxious to get involved again. The divorce made me rethink what I wanted out of life. The only person who can make me happy is me."

"Well, that's a pretty cold way to look at things," he said.

"Charlie, you're the living, breathing epitome of that philosophy. Don't deny it. Your life, up until now, has been all about you."

"So you don't think a person can change? Maybe I want to adjust my priorities."

Eve shook her head. In all her experience with men, the one thing she knew was that they didn't change. Either you learned to live with what they were or you moved on. "Of course," she lied. "People change all the time." She glanced at the clock above the sink. "I should really get home."

"It's three in the morning," he said.

"I know. But if we go back in that bedroom, we're not going to sleep. And I have a big group coming in for lunch tomorrow. I can't afford to sleep in."

"I thought we were going camping tomorrow?"

"That's going to have to wait."

He reached out and grabbed her around the waist, pulling her body against his. Charlie nuzzled her neck. "Don't go. I'll let you sleep. I promise."

"No. I think it would be good to spend the night apart." She walked toward the bedroom, collecting her clothes along the way. "I'll see you tomorrow."

She could tell he wasn't happy about her decision, but for her own self-preservation, Eve had to practice a bit of common sense. If she spent every night with him, then their relationship would be much more than she ever intended. A night in her own bed would do them both a world of good. Eve tugged on her jeans, then slipped her bare feet into her clogs.

"Come on, Eve. Don't do this," Charlie said. "This isn't some game we're playing. It's all right to admit that you enjoy sleeping with me."

"We don't do a whole lot of sleeping," she reminded him.

CHARLIE KNEW WHAT HE WAS DOING was risky. Hell, he'd spent a good portion of his lecture fee on new camping equipment and Eve hadn't really agreed to the trip. Not definitely.

He jumped out of his SUV and jogged up the front walk, then rapped on the door. A few seconds later, Lily appeared, her hair wet, a robe wrapped around her slender body. "Hi," she said.

"Is Eve here?"

"Yeah. She's in the shower. Come on in." He followed her inside. "Do you want some coffee?"

"Sure," Charlie said. He waited, pacing back and forth along the length of the living room while she fetched a mug for him.

When she returned, she gave him a wry smile. "So you gave in first. That's good. I like that. Sometimes Eve can be so stubborn. She needs a man who is willing to compromise."

"Where is the bathroom?" he asked.

"Top of the stairs on your left," Lily said.

Charlie grinned. "Thanks." He took the stairs two at a time, then slowly opened the bathroom door. The shower curtain was translucent and he watched the silhouette of Eve's naked body as she rinsed her hair.

"Do you need help washing your back?" he asked.

He saw her jump, then the shower curtain flew back and she poked her head out. Water dripped off her hair and clung to her dark lashes. "Hi," she said. "What are you doing here?"

Charlie held out the mug. "Coffee. Hurry up. We have to pack your clothes and get on the road. We're burning daylight."

"We're what?" Eve stepped out of the shower, her body glistening in the light coming through the bathroom window. Charlie bit back a groan, fighting the temptation to reach out and smooth his hand over her damp skin. In a matter of seconds, he could have his clothes off and they could get back in the shower and see what warm water and naked bodies might do.

He cleared his throat. Though he thought about sex a lot, and Eve even more, he had something different in mind for the day. "We're going camping today, remember?"

She opened her mouth, then snapped it shut. "I—I didn't think we'd finalized those plans," Eve said, reaching for a towel. "I told you we had a big group for—"

He grabbed the towel from her hands and began to dry her face. "We have to go today," Charlie said, bending down to run the towel over her legs. "I have to be back Thursday for my lecture on Friday night."

She stared at him for a long moment. "All right," she said. "Go down and tell Lily that I'm taking a few days off. I'll be ready in a half hour."

Charlie grinned. That was a lot easier than he thought it would be. He'd anticipated a series of not-so-valid excuses followed by an outright refusal to accompany him. Obviously, after their argument last night, Eve wanted to put their relationship back on track. And what better way than a night or two in the wild?

On schedule, Eve appeared a half hour later, bundled in warm clothes and carrying an overnight bag. She wore the hiking boots he'd purchased for her, along with the wool socks. "What's in the bag?" he asked.

"My stuff," she said.

"You don't need anything more that what you're wearing," he said, taking the bag from her shoulder. "In fact, you don't even need everything you're wearing."

"I at least need clean underwear," she said, bending down to rummage through the bag. She stuffed panties and a lacy bra into her jacket pocket.

"We're hiking at mid-day. It will be warm. You'd be better off in shorts and a t-shirt. Just bring a light jacket. And a pair of pants. And dry socks."

"This is exactly why we shouldn't be going," she said. "I don't even know what to wear." She began to strip off the sweater she wore. "What about pajamas?"

"We've never needed them before," he teased.

"We've never slept in the freezing cold before. I know enough to know that it's cold at night in the mountains. There's still snow up there."

"We're sticking to the foothills. The weather will be chilly, but there won't be any snow."

When she'd finally decided what to bring, Charlie gathered it up and carried it out to his SUV. He shoved it into the top compartment of his pack, then helped her into the front seat.

He headed the truck southwest, toward the Nederland area. There were plenty of places to hike and camp in the national forest and they were close enough to home in case Eve was completely miserable.

As they passed the Hotel Boulderado, a famous old Victorian-era hotel that featured luxurious rooms, Eve pointed out the window. "I'll treat," she said. "A night at the Boulderado. A soft bed, a big bathtub."

"I've spent hours in the kitchen with you," Charlie said. "Now it's time for you to see a bit more of my world."

"To what end?" she asked. "When you spend time in the kitchen with me, at least you get a meal out of it. What do I get out of this?"

"Time alone with me. In a sleeping bag. Fresh air. Exercise. Maybe we'll even see a bear."

"Except for the bear, I could get all that at the Hotel Boulderado," she said. "And I'd have a real bed."

They stopped for coffee and to Charlie's surprise, after a jolt of caffeine, Eve's mood brightened considerably. By the time they reached Nederland, she was interrogating him about the food he'd brought along and the cooking utensils she'd have available for the evening meal.

Charlie had planned the trip carefully, knowing that if he threw too much at her all at once, she'd never want to hike with him again. He'd chosen to trek along a familiar forest service road for three or four miles, then cut off on a trail that led to a flat and spacious campsite.

He wanted Eve to like this, to enjoy an outdoor adventure with him. He wanted to share the things he loved about the outdoors in the same way she shared her love of cooking with him. It was what couples were supposed to do. And more than anything, Charlie was starting to look at the two of them as a couple.

There were so many places he imagined showing her, so many cultures to eat their way through. Some of the best food he'd ever eaten was in little out-of-the-way places in exotic locations. He was beginning to imagine a life for them, all laid out in front of him. And in the same way he used to get excited about a new adventure, he was anticipating the challenges of loving Eve.

But there was one thing he worried over. Would there come a time when the excitement of being with her faded? Or would he always feel as if there was much more to explore?

They parked the truck about a mile in. Charlie handed Eve a small daypack with bottled water, protein bars and a map. Then he hauled his large pack out of the back and slipped his arms through the shoulder straps. He'd packed light and they weren't at altitude, so the hike wouldn't be difficult compared to some he'd done.

"What do you have in there?" she asked.

"Two down sleeping bags, a tent, cooking supplies,

food, your clothes, my clothes, stuff to make a fire. And two bottles of wine."

Eve shook her head in disbelief. "You're a really good packer," she said. "I have to give you that."

He slammed the cargo door on the SUV and shoved his keys in the pocket of his hiking shorts. "All right. Let's go. We're heading that way," Charlie said, pointing to the north.

It was an absolutely perfect spring day. The sun was warm and the breeze cool. They hiked at a moderate pace, chatting as they walked. For the first time since they'd met, they had a chance to really get to know each other. Without the option of jumping into bed, they could enjoy each other's company. She told him about the moment she decided to become a chef, about cooking school and about buying the Garden Gate.

They laughed and teased, falling into an easy camaraderie that Charlie had rarely found on any of his adventures. When they reached the head of the hiking trail, he asked if Eve wanted to rest, but she was willing to go on.

They reached the campsite about a half hour later, a beautiful spot set at the edge of a high meadow with the Rockies providing a perfect backdrop. Not far from the site was a river, fed from the snowmelt.

Charlie shrugged out of his pack and set it against a tree, then helped Eve out of hers. "You did well," he said.

"I'm exhausted and my feet hurt," Eve replied.

"Take off your boots and lay your socks out to dry."

She sat down on a nearby log and did as she was told. But as she pulled her socks off, she winced in pain. Charlie walked over and examined her foot, startled by the angry red blisters on her big toe and the back of her heel. He helped her out of her other boot and he found another blister on her little toe.

"Why didn't you tell me your feet hurt?" he asked.

"I really didn't notice until now. They're just blisters."

"They're going to be even more painful on the walk out," he said.

She laughed. "I'm a lot tougher than you think I am."

Charlie gave her a wary look. "You sit. I'm going to set up the tent. Then I'll go get some water. You can soak your feet and they'll feel much better."

As he pulled the poles for the tent out of the pack, Charlie glanced over at Eve. He'd always had just one person to worry about on his adventures—himself. But now that Eve was with him, he needed to be more careful.

Hell, there were a million and one things that could hurt you in the woods—bears, mountain lions, rattle-snakes. A simple fall could kill you. He felt uneasy about the responsibility. Yet there was no one else he'd rather have looking after Eve than himself.

When he finished setting up the tent, he stepped back and pointed to it with a flourish. "Home, sweet home," he said.

Eve laughed. "That barely looks big enough for one person, let alone two."

"We don't need much room," he said. "It's not that much smaller than my bed and we get along fine there." He held out his hand. "Come on. Let me give you a tour."

She stood up and gingerly walked across the hard-packed ground. They both crawled inside and Charlie leaned back, bracing his elbows behind him. "This is the bedroom," he said. "And the living room. The kitchen is out there. As is the bathroom. The bathtub is down by the river."

"It's a lovely home," Eve said, turning to him and placing a soft kiss on his lips. "And you built it just for me."

"Some day I'll build you a bigger and better one, I promise."

Eve looked around. "I kind of like this one," she said. She pushed him back then crawled on top of him, tossing her jacket aside. "Maybe we ought to break it in?"

Charlie growled playfully as he pulled her into a long deep kiss. "We are in the bedroom, after all."

EVE SAT NEXT TO THE FIRE, wrapped in Charlie's sleeping bag, her chin resting on her knees. Sparks drifted upward on the night breeze, disappearing overheard into the starry sky. "I love this," Eve murmured.

Charlie glanced up from tending the fire. "What?"

"I love that you brought me here. I didn't think I'd like it, but I do. It's so peaceful. I haven't thought about the restaurant since we left Boulder. How is that possible? I think about the restaurant all the time."

"What were you thinking about?" he asked.

"You." Eve didn't think it was wrong to admit the truth. "How strange it is that you came back into my life. How it seems like only yesterday that you left. And how funny it is that we picked up right where we left off."

"Things are different," he said. "We're both a little older and a little wiser."

"I guess so," Eve replied. Was that a good thing? Somehow, Eve didn't think that her divorce had improved her attitude about love and commitment.

"Do you want to talk about what happened last night? Why you got so angry with me?" Charlie asked.

"I just don't think we should talk about the future," Eve said. "I want to enjoy the present, this moment, right now. And I want you to know that when you leave again, I'll be all right."

"You'd be all right if I left next week?"

Eve nodded. She would. But there was one ca-veat. "As long you as you promised that you'd come back."

"When?"

"I don't know. Whenever."

Charlie shook his head. "You'd be fine with that. If I just wandered off for a year and then came back."

Eve nodded. "I would. It's who you are, Charlie. And I think I need to accept that. You'll drift in and out of my life and we'll be together when we can. It wouldn't be so bad."

He gave her an odd look, as if he didn't find the idea all that appealing. What wasn't to like? He could have his cake and eat it, too. She was giving him per-mission to be exactly who he was. And in turn, she'd have the freedom to do what she wanted.

He walked over to his pack, which he'd braced against a tree, then withdrew a plastic bag and tossed it her way. "Dessert," he said, indicating the bag of marshmallows. "But don't drop any around the camp-site. Bears love them."

"I haven't had roasted marshmallows since I was a kid. God, I'd kill for some chocolate bars and graham crackers."

"I have those, too," Charlie said, walking back to where she sat with another plastic bag. He reached behind her and grabbed a green branch he'd stripped earlier. "There are some nice embers in the fire."

"Tell me about your next adventure," Eve said as she stuck a pair of marshmallows on the stick.

"It's going to be something completely different," Charlie said. "Something I've never tried before."

"Where are you going?"

"I'm not sure yet. But you'll be the first to know."

Well, at least she'd get fair warning and be able to prepare herself, she thought. "We really shouldn't eat dessert before we have dinner," Eve said, quickly changing the subject.

"You ate an entire bag of granola," he said. "And you're still hungry?"

Eve laughed. "All this fresh air does make me think about eating." She watched as Charlie pulled the marshmallows out of the fire. They were perfectly brown and gooey. She held out a graham cracker topped with a piece of chocolate, then put the hot marshmallows on top. Sandwiched between another graham cracker, it made the perfect treat.

"Here," she said, holding it out to him. "Try it."

"You first," Charlie said.

Eve took a bite and the marshmallow dripped down her chin. Charlie leaned close and licked the sticky mess away, then let his mouth drift over her lips. He kissed her softly. "Take your clothes off," he murmured. "I want to make love to you under the stars."

"It's cold," she whispered.

"I'll keep you warm." He pulled the sleeping bag down over her shoulder, then exposed a tiny bit of skin. His lips and tongue were warm and she felt a rush of desire course through her body. He took her hand and drew her to her feet, then spread the sleeping bag out on a spot near the fire.

Slowly, Charlie undressed her. Her skin prickled with goose bumps, but she didn't feel the cold. Instead, the cold seemed to heighten the sensation of his touch and she found herself craving the warmth of his hands as she never had before.

When she was naked, Charlie stripped out of his own clothes, then pulled her down onto the sleeping bag. This all felt so strange, Eve thought. She felt all the baggage of her past just disappear in the dark. This was simple and primal, lust and longing in its most basic form.

She pressed him back against the ground, then straddled his hips. His erection, already fully aroused, rested against the damp spot between her legs. She moved against him, tipped her head back and closed her eyes.

He found her breasts, her nipples hard from the cold, and he teased until she ached with desire. Eve wanted him inside her without anything between them. After her divorce, she continued to take her birth control pills, thinking that any day, she'd need them again. That day had finally come.

She reached down and guided him into the depths of her warmth. At first, he seemed to resist, but then Charlie accepted her silent invitation. Slowly, she came down on top of him, until there was nowhere left to move.

Eve sighed, a smile curling the corners of her mouth. Had this ever felt so good? So perfect? She couldn't imagine anyone else in the world affecting her the way Charlie did. When he moved inside her, she was completely free to feel, to experience every shade and hue of her desire.

The light from the fire cast his profile in soft relief and she watched the interplay of pleasure and anticipation on his features. His eyes were closed, his jaw set, as if he was trying to delay the inevitable.

Eve knew there wasn't much in this relationship that she could control. He would come and go as he pleased. But she could make him wait, make him beg for his release. She slowed her pace, rising up on her knees until he was nearly free of her warmth before plunging back down again.

He opened his eyes and looked at her, surprised by what she was doing. Eve smiled, then bent down and kissed him. Charlie was right. There was a something beautiful about making love outdoors. She felt completely exposed, her emotions laid bare for him to see.

If she didn't love him now, Eve knew it was only a matter of time. How could she resist a man who made her believe in the possibilities of a future? She wasn't sure she could save herself from another round of heartache and disappointment. But there were moments, like this one, when all the heartache would be worth it.

When he moved to touch her at the spot where they were joined, Eve grabbed his hands and pinned them on either side of his head. She was going to control this one small thing. She was going to make him want her as much as she wanted him.

And in the end, he gave in to the pleasure she offered. But to Eve's surprise, the seduction was more than she could handle. His soft whispers sent her over the edge and she collapsed against his chest in a string of delicious spasms.

He wrapped them both in the sleeping bag, drawing her tight against his warm body. Eve sighed softly, snuggling into the curve of his arm. "You were right," she whispered.

"About what?"

"I need to get outside more and get some exercise," she said. "I feel so much better already."

Charlie chuckled, pressing a kiss to the top of her head. "This isn't exactly what I was thinking about. And it's not something you can do in Boulder."

"It might be kind of fun," she said. "Sneaking around looking for places we can be alone."

He drew back and looked into her eyes. "Really? 'Cause I know a few spots."

She reached down and smoothed her hand over his belly. "We wouldn't have to stay in town. I think I should take a bit more time for myself. I work hard. I deserve a break every now and then." She smiled. "So where should we go next?"

"You know where I'd love to take you? India. No, Turkey. And then Nepal. And China."

"I was thinking about Estes Park," Eve said. "But I've always wanted to see the Great Wall. And there's a lot of vegetarian cooking in China. I do a lot of Asian-influenced cooking. I'd love to go to Thailand."

"We'll go there first," Charlie said. "You'll love it."

"Hmm," she said. It was a nice diversion to dream about such things. But Eve knew that the chances of them traveling to Thailand were slim at best. She had a restaurant to run, he had his work.

"I'm not just blowing smoke here," Charlie said. "I'm serious. I think we should travel."

"I thought we discussed this," Eve said. "It really isn't good to make promises we can't keep."

"I'm not making a promise. We get along well and I'm tired of traveling alone. I think you'd make a good companion."

"I'd want to spend all my time in restaurants," she said.

"I have to eat. And I'd want to spend my time seeing the countryside."

"I need exercise," she countered.

"See? We'd make the perfect pair."

Eve closed her eyes and curled more deeply into his embrace. They did make a good pair. But as nice as that felt now, Eve knew this infatuation would fade over time. Sooner or later, they'd have to deal with the realities of their relationship. The impossibilities would overwhelm the potential.

She sighed, her breath clouding in the chilly air. There was no predicting when the end would come or how it would happen. But Eve already knew how she'd feel. He'd always be the one that got away, the one she could have loved.

5

"I JUST NEED A LITTLE ADVICE," Charlie said. "I thought I'd start with the appliances."

They stood in the kitchen of the Garden Gate, Charlie sitting on the edge of the prep table and Eve moving easily around the kitchen.

After their night in the wild, Charlie had noticed a subtle change in Eve. She was a bit more distant, more introverted. The sex was still incredible, but he felt as though she were pulling away.

He could guess what she was worried about. The more time they spent together, the more it became apparent that he and Eve belonged together. But convincing her to see the possibilities would be difficult. He had a lousy track record with women. And it wasn't something he was proud of. But a guy could change...if he really wanted to.

"That's not how you design a new kitchen," Eve said. "First you figure out the layout and outline the work areas. Then you pick out cabinetry and countertops and flooring. And then, you decide on the appliances."

Charlie flipped through the catalog. "This is why I need help." In truth, it was important that Eve like his kitchen. He was renovating it for her. If things continued to go well between them, then she'd be spending all her time at his place. He wanted her to feel at home there.

"Maybe if you told me what you want out of your kitchen, I could give you better advice. Do you plan to do a lot of gourmet cooking or are you more of a thirty-minute meal kind of guy? Are you looking for something that looks fancy or do you want functional?"

"Yes," he said.

"Yes to what?"

"All of it. I want to make it something a professional, like yourself, would enjoy working in. Why don't you come home with me and we can discuss all of these points in greater detail?"

She regarded him suspiciously. "I know what you're doing," she said, waving a wire whisk at him. "This isn't about your kitchen. This is about your…" She pointed to his crotch. "Utensil. I have work to do. I'm doing a cooking segment on a morning news show next week and I have to be ready."

"You're going to be on television?" he asked, grabbing a peeled carrot from a nearby bowl. He took a bite, then chewed slowly. "Cool. Are you going to wear that hat? 'Cause it doesn't do you any favors."

She snatched off the toque and tossed it aside. "In fact, I might have my own cooking show. I've had a couple of offers, one from PBS and another from the Food Channel."

When he'd first met Eve, she'd been a hired chef at the Garden Gate. Now, she owned the place, had written a vegetarian cookbook and was considering television offers. She'd become a different person in five years, at least on the outside. She had people depending upon her and important things to do. And all he cared about was luring her back into bed.

"We can talk about this later," he said, closing the appliance brochure and pushing it aside. "I'll let you get back to work. I'll see you when you get home." He turned for the door, but she reached out to stop him.

"I was just going to walk down to the farmer's market. Do you want to come with me?"

"You want me to come vegetable shopping with you?" Charlie asked. "Wow, I've had some thrills in my life, but I'm not sure I can handle something that intense. Are we just going to be buying green vegetables, or will there be other colors, too?"

Eve groaned, shaking her head. "They sell more than veggies there. There's a really great Mexican food stand at the market and they make the best corn tamales. We could have lunch." She paused.

"And then, I suppose I might want to take a nap afterward."

"I could use a nap." *Nap.* That had become their euphemism for sex in the middle of the day. They'd spent most of yesterday afternoon "napping," after they returned from camping.

Though he needed to start going over his notes for the lectures he'd be giving tomorrow night, Charlie was more than happy to be distracted by her naked body in his bed.

Eve slipped out of her white chef's jacket, then grabbed her sweater from the desk in the corner of the kitchen. "Grab those bags," she said. "I've got the list."

When they stepped out onto the street, the mid-morning sun was warm and the breeze gentle. Spring-time in Boulder was his favorite time of the year. And he was glad he'd chosen to spend it with Eve. He grabbed her hand and when she looked over at him, he smiled. "Do you have a problem with this?" he said.

"A public display of affection usually requires an explanation."

"Do you really think we'll need one?"

She shrugged. "I know a lot of people in this town. I haven't been dating. Someone is surely going to be curious. What am I supposed to tell them?"

"Tell them I'm your boyfriend," he said.

"Charlie, I—"

He turned and grabbed her face in his hands, then kissed her, lingering over her mouth for much longer than he should have, his tongue teasing at her lips provocatively. If she was worried about public displays of affection, she needn't bother. He'd just given the crowd a public display of naked lust. "I'm your boyfriend, Eve. That's all there is to it. We have a romantic relationship. I don't know where the hell it's going, but that doesn't matter. Now, just say it."

"Say what?" she asked breathlessly.

"Say, 'Charlie, you are my boyfriend.'"

"Charlie, you are my boyfriend."

"There, that wasn't so hard, was it?"

She shook her head. "I guess not."

"So, now we can hold hands. We're officially going together."

"This sounds like high school," Eve commented wryly.

"Maybe that's where we should start."

"I think we've gotten a little ahead ourselves. What we've been doing wasn't even a possibility in high school. I was a very naive girl. I didn't even know that tongues were involved in kissing until I was a junior in high school." She paused. "But then, I suppose you were quite the Casanova."

Charlie shook his head. "Actually, no. I didn't lose my virginity until I was a sophomore in college. I didn't spend a lot of time with girls in high school. I was too busy climbing rocks and kayaking down rivers. Girls really didn't like to do that stuff, so until I had my first sexual experience, I didn't have much use for them."

"And then?"

"And then I realized how much fun they were," Charlie said.

"And then you had a lot of sex," she said.

"And then, I realized that a lot of sex wasn't necessarily a good thing. When I came back to Boulder, I realized there's a lot more to like about a woman than what you experience in the bedroom."

"And what do you like about me?" Eve asked, turning to face him.

He slipped his arm around her shoulder and pulled her close. "I like that you want me to eat better. And that you fold up my clothes when I throw them on the floor. I like how you look when you wear my T-shirt, and only my T-shirt, to make us breakfast. And I love the way you smell when you come out of the shower."

She seemed taken aback by his rhapsodizing. A pretty blush stained her cheeks and she turned away to stare into a shop window. When she turned back to him, she smiled. "I'm hungry. Are you?"

Maybe he had been a bit too open about his feelings for her, but Charlie was sick of playing games. He liked Eve, a lot more than he'd ever liked any woman before. Hell, he might even love her, though he wasn't sure he'd recognize the feeling if he did.

There was absolutely nothing wrong with telling her what was on his mind.

"Eve!"

A man's voice brought them both to a stop at the entrance to the farmer's market. He heard Eve's voice catch in her throat and she cursed softly.

"What?" Charlie said.

"It's Dave," she said. "My ex."

"Matt," Charlie corrected.

"Dave, Matt, it doesn't make a difference what I call him. He's coming over here right now. I really don't want to talk to him."

"Then don't," Charlie said.

Charlie had never formally met Matt, though he'd seen him once, five years ago, chatting with Eve in front of her restaurant. The guy looked like an accountant, all buttoned-up and business-like, his hair trimmed short and his shirt pressed perfectly. Charlie didn't like him for a myriad of reasons, the primary one being that he'd swooped in and married Eve when she'd been most vulnerable. Charlie cursed inwardly. But then, whose fault was that?

"Hello, Eve," Matt said.

"Hi." She forced a smile.

"I'm glad we ran into each other. I just wanted to let you know that I met with my lawyer yesterday. I've decided to move ahead with what we discussed."

"Discussed?" Charlie said, glancing between the two of them. "What did you discuss?"

"Nothing," Eve said.

Matt sent Charlie a dismissive glance. "Who is your friend?"

"I'm not her friend," Charlie said. "I'm her boyfriend. Charlie Templeton." He didn't bother holding out his hand in greeting. He was afraid to move his arm, afraid he might just deck the guy right in the middle of a crowd of onlookers.

"You didn't mention you were involved, Eve," Matt said, an uneasy look on his face.

"It's none of your business," Eve said. "If you'll excuse us, we're going to lunch." She grabbed Charlie's arm and pulled him along the sidewalk. "Ugh, he just makes me so angry."

"What was that thing about his lawyer?"

"He wants to renegotiate our divorce settlement. I bought him out of his share of the restaurant. Now that the restaurant is making money and I've got some other things going on, he thinks he was cheated. He thinks he deserves more."

"Would you like me to go punch him in the face?" Charlie asked, hoping she'd agree.

"No. Don't bother. He's not worth it."

"There is one good thing I can say for the guy," Charlie murmured. "He was too stupid to realize what he had when he married you. If it wasn't for that, you two might still be married. And I wouldn't have a girlfriend."

"And there is the fact that he thought the restaurant

would fail without his considerable skills as a businessman. He thought he was getting the better end of the deal when we settled." She pointed to a small stand. "There it is. Come on. You'll love this place. The food is healthy and your insides will thank you."

Charlie wanted to question her more about her ex, but he could see how eager she was to change the subject. There would be plenty of time to learn all the details later. And if the guy got too pushy, Charlie would just have to invite him out for a beer and a little talk.

He smiled to himself as he listened to Eve order the corn tamales. There was a certain pleasure in watching over her, in protecting her. Though Eve could certainly take care of herself, he wanted to be there, to give support when she needed it.

After all, that's what a boyfriend did. And he was now, officially, Eve Keller's boyfriend.

"Hey, Charlie!"

Charlie glanced up from his notes to see Kevin Martin strolling down the aisle of the lecture hall. He'd just finished the first of his talks and it had gone better than he'd expected, considering he hadn't spent a lot of time preparing. The lecture hall had been full and the crowd enthusiastic.

Kevin was a friend he'd met on his climb of Mount Vinson in Antarctica. Now he ran a sports marketing firm and had been booking Charlie's speaking engagements and media appearances for the past two years.

"Kevin. What are you doing here?"

"I've got the family over at Breckinridge for some spring skiing and I thought I'd drive over and see your presentation. And, I'm bringing some good news."

Charlie gathered up his laptop and his notes and tucked them under his arm. "What kind of news?"

"I got a call a few days ago from National Geographic. I sent them a reel of some of your appearances and they want you to host a special. About the ecological impact of climbing expeditions on Everest. It's all part of a yearlong push they're doing on the environment. They're funding the whole thing. You'll prep with the production company in Boston starting next week and then spend a month on site filming in May."

"Why so soon? How are they going to put it all together that quickly?" Charlie paused, then nodded. "I'm not their first choice, am I?"

Kevin shook his head. "No. They had Dirk Phillips but he had to back out at the last minute. He broke his leg mountain biking and hasn't fully recovered. Your climbing permit is still good, so you made an attractive substitute."

"I don't know," Charlie said. "I just got back from Everest. I'm still recovering from jet lag. Two climbs in one season is crazy."

"You'll have a huge support staff. And they don't expect you to summit. You'll film around base camp and advance base camp, interview the Sherpas, the local government officials, the climbing guides. You'll do most of that in Katmandu as they come off the mountain."

Charlie knew this was an incredible opportunity. National Geographic was the pinnacle of the industry. Their expeditions were perfectly run, with personnel who knew exactly what they were doing. And if he took this job, there might be others in the future.

As much as he wanted to stay with Eve, he had to find a way to make a living. He couldn't depend upon her to pay the bills. And this was only for a month. "Do I have some time to think about it?"

Kevin held out a piece of paper. "Take a look at this. It's the compensation package they're offering. I don't think you need to think. This kind of salary puts you in a whole different ballpark."

"Why me?"

"Look at yourself, Charlie. Guys want to be your best friend and women want to sleep with you. You have a face made for television. I'm just surprised no one has noticed before."

"Okay," Charlie said. "I'll think about it. I'll call you in a few days."

"They need to know by Tuesday or they'll push everything back to next season. And then Dirk will be available," Kevin said. He smiled. "Nice job on the speech. Television is going to love you."

Charlie wandered back to the area they'd designated as his dressing room. It wasn't more than an empty office with an adjacent bathroom. He sat down on the edge of a table. The offer was too good to pass up. Even he could see that.

But was he ready to walk out on Eve? Things were just starting to go well. If was really committed to changing his life, then there shouldn't be any second thoughts. He ought to want to stay in Boulder.

Yet there it was, that old familiar pull. That anticipation, that curiosity, that undeniable need to see what was waiting for him around the next corner. The urge to wander wasn't nearly as strong, but it was still there.

Charlie cursed softly. He couldn't continue to do this for the rest of his life. Sooner or later, he'd realize that he didn't have a life. He rubbed his face with his hands, trying to clear his head and make sense of all these feelings.

"Charlie Templeton?"

Charlie opened his eyes to find a beautiful woman standing at the door. Great. This was all he needed. He waited for the attraction to hit, but to his surprise, he felt nothing. She was exactly the kind of woman he had always been attracted to—blonde and willowy. "That's me," he said. "What can I do for you?"

She held out her hand. "My name is Angela

Weatherby. I was wondering if you'd have time for an interview?"

"I'm kind of in a—"

"It won't take long. I just have a few questions."

What was the harm? He felt no attraction at all. And professionally, he ought to spend more time getting his name out. "Sure," he said, shaking her hand. There it was again. No reaction to touching her. He grabbed a chair and pulled it out for her. "Sit. So, who do you work for?"

She forced a smile. "Actually, I work for myself. I have a blog and a Web site. But my questions are for a book I'm writing."

"About climbing?" She didn't exactly look like she spent a lot of time outdoors. Her nails were too well manicured and her skin was pale and unlined.

"Not exactly."

"So, what would you like to ask?"

"First, I want to assure you that your interview will be strictly anonymous. Protecting your real identity will be my first priority. I want you to speak freely."

He frowned. Why would he want to do an anonymous interview? He didn't have any secrets. "I don't understand. What is this about?"

"When did you first notice girls?" Angela asked, her digital recorder poised to capture his answer.

"What?"

"I'm interested in understanding the process. How

does one go from ordinary kid to ladies' man? Exactly who taught you how to seduce women? Was it something you just picked up by trial and error or did you have a mentor?"

"What is this? A joke? I think you have me confused with someone else," he said, getting to his feet.

"I run a Web site called SmoothOperators.com and you have a very large profile with us. You've dated a lot of women and fifteen of them have written comments about you. I'd like to talk to you about that, about your relationships with women."

Charlie stared at her for a long moment. "I'm on a Web site?"

"Yes," she said. "SmoothOperators.com."

He grabbed his laptop and turned it on, then waited for a wireless connection. When he found one, he handed the laptop to Angela. "Show me."

She typed in the Web address, then flipped through a few links. When she was finished, she handed him the computer. To Charlie's shock, he saw a photo of himself and an entire list of posts from women he'd slept with. "Shit," he murmured. "Can anyone see this?"

She nodded. "Yes. If they know where to look. Your profile doesn't come up on a search, though. You have to enter our site first."

"And this is legal?"

"Oh, yes."

Charlie read through some of the comments, wincing as he came across passages he recognized. He glanced up at the first post. "VeggieLuv," he murmured. It certainly didn't take a rocket scientist to figure that one out. Slowly, a memory crystallized in his mind.

That first night in the restaurant, Eve had mentioned something about a Web site, then quickly changed the subject. Was this what she'd been talking about? Is that why she thought he'd returned, to exact some punishment for posting the profile?

Eve's post was long and detailed and horribly unflattering. This is what she really thought of him, Charlie mused. No wonder she was so wary about starting a relationship. He was exactly the kind of man she wanted to avoid. "So, I've dated a lot of women. I'm a single guy. There's no law against that."

"No, there isn't. And I'm not interested in admonishing you for your skills in seducing women. I'm interested in finding out why and how you got this way. I want to explain to women what makes a drifter, like you, tick."

"A drifter?"

"Yes. That's your archetype. You move from place to place, never settling down. You lead women to believe they may just have what it takes to make you commit. And when you get bored, you move on."

"Back up a second, here. I never made any promises."

"Exactly!" Angela said. "That's exactly what I expected you to say. But how do you think that makes women feel?"

He stood up, shaking his head. "I don't know what to say. I'm sorry if I acted like an ass. Write that on your Web site or in your book. I'm doing my best to make some changes in my life. And now, I really have to go."

With that, he grabbed his jacket and his computer and walked out of the room. Angela hurried after him. "I really would like to speak to you in more detail," she called. "Could I phone you?"

Charlie strode down the hall, then shoved open the door and stepped out into the cool spring night. Maybe he'd been fooling himself all along. Perhaps Angela Weatherby knew him better than he knew himself. And Eve knew him best of all.

"THE RASPBERRY AND RADISH salad was huge tonight," Lily said, flipping through the dinner tickets. "The mushroom and leek tartlet went well, too. And that lavender ice cream with a pear crumble was incredible. You have to put those recipes in the new book."

"I haven't had a chance to even think about the new book."

"You have been a bit distracted," Lily said. "So, how are things going with the new man? Or would he be the new old man?"

"I have no idea what or who he is," Eve said.

"Sometimes, I really wish I could go back to the way things were before he showed up for lunch. My life was so simple. I could focus on my cooking." She closed her eyes and groaned. "I am so confused." She looked at Lily. "Do I really want a man in my life right now?"

"Of course you do," Lily said. "Especially that man." She reached out and rubbed Eve's shoulder. "Eve, you need to relax and let things unfold naturally. I know you like to plan, but a relationship is not like a recipe. No matter how hard you try to control the ingredients, it's never going to come out perfect in the end. But that doesn't mean it can't be delicious."

A shiver skittered down Eve's spine. It was delicious already. Every moment she spent with Charlie was suffused with desire. No matter what they were doing, all she had to do was reach out and touch him and she was reminded of what they shared in the bedroom.

She'd never been with a man who'd made her feel so sexual. And when she was with him, she felt energized, alive, like she could conquer the world. And yet, she felt that same nervous energy that she had when her marriage was falling apart—the need to control every facet of the relationship.

If only she could follow Lily's advice—to just let go and allow her emotions to lead her. She recalled a comment that one of her mentors at culinary school had given her. Unless she invested her heart and soul in her cooking, there would always be something missing from her plate.

"Chef?"

Sarah stood in the kitchen door. "What's up?" Eve asked.

"Charlie is out front. He wants to talk to you."

"Tell him to come in," Eve said.

"He said he needed to talk to you outside."

Eve frowned. "All right." No doubt, he wanted her alone for a few minutes. Although, why he couldn't wait an hour until she got home, Eve didn't know. She walked through the main dining room and then into the bar. His silhouette was visible through the plate glass window at the front of the restaurant.

She paused for a moment, noting the tense set of his shoulders. He was pacing back and forth from the door to the street. Drawing a deep breath, she pulled the bandanna off her head and set it on the bar.

As Eve stepped out into the cool night, she ruffled her short-cropped hair. "I thought we were going to meet at your place after your speech," Eve said.

He turned to face her. Eve's breath caught in her throat. It was clear he was angry. But beyond that, she saw something else in his eyes. Hurt? Indecision? Regret? What was it?

"You're VeggieLuv, aren't you?" he asked, walking toward her.

Eve heard a gasp slip from her lips and she quickly

scrambled for an explanation. Though the Web site was easy to access, what were the chances that he'd stumble upon it by himself? Someone must have told him. But who?

"Are you?" Charlie asked. He held up his hand, silencing her reply. "Never mind. You don't need to tell me. It's good to know how you really feel about me."

"How I felt," Eve said. "Past tense. I wrote that a year ago. After my divorce. And after a very large bottle of wine and a big dose of self-pity."

"You know what? You're right. You were right about it all. I can't commit. I can't bring myself to consider the possibility that there might be just one woman out there for me. One woman who I'll spend the rest of my life loving."

"I never asked you for a commitment," Eve said. "Just the opposite. You are who you are, and I've accepted that."

"Don't," he said. "Because the guy I used to be was a first-rate ass." He raked his hands through his hair. "But it's really good to know how you feel about me."

"That was then," Eve said. "My feelings have changed…considerably."

"How considerably?" he demanded.

"A lot," she said. "I understand now why you had to leave and I don't blame you. It was my fault. I wanted a commitment and you weren't ready for that.

I knew that going in but I thought I could change you. That's what every woman thinks. But I was wrong."

"So you wanted to make me a better man?"

"Yes," she said. Eve sighed. "No. Just my version of a good man. But don't you see, we're both in the same place now? That's good, right?"

"And what place is that?"

"Neither one of us is looking for anything permanent. We're just going to enjoy ourselves for as long as you stay and when it's time to say goodbye, there will be no regrets."

Charlie stared at her for a long moment, then cursed softly. "I gotta go. I'll talk to you later." He turned and strode down the sidewalk, not bothering to look back.

"Come on, Charlie," Eve called. "Don't be angry. It was a stupid thing for me to do. I'm sorry."

He disappeared around a corner and Eve groaned softly. In all the time they'd spent together, they'd never fought. There were so many better ways to occupy their time. What did this mean? People fought when they actually had a relationship. All his talk about boyfriend and girlfriend was just teasing… wasn't it?

"What are you doing out here?"

Eve turned to find Lily standing in the door of the restaurant. "Nothing."

Lily glanced up and down the street. "Where is Charlie?"

"He left."

"Left? Like, gone? Gone for good?"

Eve shrugged, tears pressing at the corners of her eyes. She brushed them away in frustration. This was crazy. What was she crying over? "I don't know. He's mad about that profile I posted on SmoothOperators.com. Or maybe not. He just yelled some stuff and then stormed off."

"Are you crying?" Lily asked, hurrying to her side. "Oh, Eve, I'm so sorry."

"Don't be," she said through her tears. A giggle burst from her lips. "I'm fine. Really. I kept my heart out of this. I don't love him."

But that wasn't exactly the truth, Eve thought to herself. She did have feelings for him, feelings she was afraid to admit to herself. He was everything she'd ever wanted in a man. He was sweet and funny and made her feel special, as if she were the only person in the world he ever wanted.

But how much of that was just an illusion, a practiced facade that he'd used on other women? Even through her infatuation, Eve knew that there was a chance she was just fooling herself. Men didn't change. It was an axiom that had held true for ages. A woman could either accept a man, flaws and all, or move on.

She'd already made enough concessions in her

marriage to Matt. Putting up with his behavior had been enough to sour her optimism about love and fidelity. Why even attempt to redeem her faith in the opposite sex? She'd only get her heart broken all over again.

"For someone who isn't in love, you sure look miserable," Lily teased. "Come on inside. We'll sit down and have a glass of wine."

Eve shook her head. "Can you finish up? I'm going to take a walk and clear my head. I'll be back to close up."

"I can come with you," Lily offered. "We can take our wine in a to-go cup."

"No, I'll be fine." She gave Lily's arm a squeeze. "Really, I'm great. I have everything under control."

Eve started off down the street at a brisk pace. The evening was cool and quiet, a welcome respite from the noise and heat in the kitchen. She glanced up at the sky and noticed the stars twinkling through the light from the city. Her mind wandered back to the night she and Charlie had spent camping.

Everything was so easy between them when they rid themselves of all expectations. In truth, Eve could see the allure of living a rootless life, never knowing exactly where you were going to be from day to day, always surprised by what was around the next corner.

Maybe that's what was needed to keep passion

alive between two people—that niggling doubt that tomorrow it might all be over. She didn't want to settle in to a relationship, she wanted to live and breathe her desires. She wanted a man who never stopped surprising her.

By the time Eve had exhausted herself, she realized that she was just a block from Charlie's house. Standing on the street corner, the wind rustling the trees above her head, Eve weighed her options. She could walk back to the restaurant and keep her pride intact. Or she could go to Charlie, apologize for ratting him out online and see what she could do the fix the mess she'd made.

There was a third option. She could let herself in, take off all her clothes and wait in his bed. If he just remembered how good it was between them, then he'd have to see how misplaced his anger was.

Eve leaned up against the tree, wrapping her arms around herself to ward off the chill in the air. There would come a point when sex couldn't fix every problem they had. Maybe they were at that point now. Maybe it was just best to let it go, before either of them invested too much.

Still, no matter what happened in the future, Eve wanted to set things straight in the present. She stepped back out on the sidewalk and headed in the direction of Charlie's house. Now that he'd had a chance to calm down, maybe he'd listen to her side of the story.

The house was dark as she walked up the front steps to the porch. There was always a key hidden on a string behind the mailbox, but Eve decided to knock. She held her arm out, then hesitated, knowing she ought to decide what to say first. The sight of Charlie usually rendered her unable to think clearly.

"Tell him you're sorry," she murmured. "And that it was a long time ago, before you really knew him."

She reached out again, but then another thought occurred to her. She really shouldn't have to apologize. After all, Charlie had admitted he had behaved like an ass. And nothing she'd written on the Web site was untrue.

Gathering her resolve, Eve rapped on the door, then waited. She listened for sounds inside, but heard nothing. Pressing her hands to the glass in the door, she peered into the darkness. Maybe he'd already gone to bed. Or maybe he hadn't come home at all.

She grabbed the key from its spot and unlocked the door, then slowly pushed it open. Her eyes adjusted to the light and she walked into the living room. Eve's breath caught as she saw him, sitting on the floor, his back against the leather sofa.

"You didn't answer," she murmured.

6

HE CLOSED HIS EYES, the sound of her voice sending a sweet surge of desire through his body. No matter how hard he tried to convince himself otherwise, the feelings he had for Eve were more than just superficial. She'd managed to wiggle her way into his life, carving out a place in his heart that would be left empty if she abandoned him.

But she'd made her feelings very clear. She wasn't interested in anything beyond a sexual relationship. What they shared in bed was incredibly powerful. Yet the past few nights, he'd found himself searching for more, a closeness that could only come with complete honesty.

"Listen, I know you're angry," she began. "But you have to understand how hurt I was. And it really wasn't about you, it was about Matt. I wrote all of that after the divorce hearing, after fighting with him over money, after learning about all the cheating."

She slowly crossed the room and sat down beside him. Even from a few feet away, he could feel the warmth of her body, smell the scent of her shampoo. Charlie clenched his fingers into fists, trying to fight the impulse to yank her into his arms and kiss her. Kissing her would set everything right again, at least for the moment. And it would probably evolve into a full-scale seduction, which would make them both forget the anger between them.

Sex had always been the answer for him. Whatever ailment he wanted to cure, finding a warm and willing woman was the first prescription he took. But he sensed that they'd moved past using sex as a salve.

When he touched her, it meant something more than just a means to eventual release. Every caress had become a promise, every kiss a silent question. What did it all mean? Was he really falling in love?

Charlie glanced over at Eve. She sat silently beside him, staring into the cold fireplace. "I'm not angry at you," he said. "I'm mad at myself. I thought I had things exactly how I wanted them. And now, I realize I didn't know what I wanted."

"It's not supposed to be easy," she said, turning to face him. Her fingertips smoothed over his lips and she leaned forward to kiss him. "I don't want to fight with you."

Charlie slipped his fingers through the hair at her nape and pulled her toward him for a long, deep kiss. He searched for her taste, that wonderful sweetness that had become as addictive as a drug to him. And when he found it, Charlie felt himself relax, as if his last care in the world had suddenly dissolved.

Eve's hands moved to the buttons of his shirt and it took her only a few seconds before she was pushing it off his shoulders and smoothing her palms over his torso. If her taste wasn't enough to fire his passion, then her touch was. She knew his body so well, all the most sensitive spots, the places she'd claimed as her own.

Charlie didn't know how they'd managed to shed their clothes. He was only aware of her naked flesh beneath his hands. Before he knew it, they were both undressed and lying on the rug in the middle of the room.

Her fingers encircled his cock, stroking slowly, teasing him to full arousal. He kept his mind occupied with a slow trail of kisses from the base of her throat to her breasts and then back again. His release was already so close… The need to let go was building up inside him.

When she sat up and straddled his hips, he thought that she was ready to join him. But slowly, she drifted lower, her lips pressed against his chest and then his belly and then beyond.

A raw moan tore from his throat as she took him in her mouth. He used to look on this act as just a means to an end, the perfect orgasm. But with Eve, Charlie felt as if she were testing his need, forcing him to be vulnerable to the feel of her lips and tongue on his shaft.

He could surrender to her, completely and without hesitation. Though they'd only been together ten days and nights, it felt like longer, as if the trust they shared had grown over time. Charlie felt his breath quicken in response to her pace and he fought back the need to surrender. Still, Eve grew more determined, each stroke, each caress bringing him closer to the edge.

There would come a time, when he was alone in his tent on the side of some distant mountain, when he'd remember every detail of this. When the mere recollection would send him over the edge. For now, he had real pleasure, not imagined.

"I'm so close," he murmured.

"What do you want?" Eve asked, looking up at him with a lazy smile. "Do you want me to stop?"

Charlie nodded. But when a frown wrinkled her brow he chuckled softly. "I want you to stop that and start something else." Gently, he grabbed her arms and drew her alongside him. And then, holding on to her waist, he rolled on top of her and buried himself to the hilt.

It happened so quickly, the shift of power, his cock sliding inside her, that she gasped. Slowly, he began to move, her warmth enveloping him until he lost the ability to think. Instinct took over and they grasped at each other, as if they were both unable to get close enough.

And then, she was there, at the edge one moment and dissolving into spasms the next. Charlie arched against her and let himself go, each thrust taking him to a more perfect place.

When they'd both regained their breath, Charlie stretched out beside her, throwing his leg over her thighs and his arm around her waist. It had all happened so quickly. He was used to taking more time with her.

He waited for the contentment to set in, waited for that long, slow descent into complete relaxation. But it didn't come. Just like on Everest, he felt incomplete. There were words on the tip of his tongue, words that needed to be said, but Charlie was afraid that telling her how he really felt might drive her away for good.

He sat up and ran his hands through his hair. Her hand smoothed down his back. "That was nice," she murmured.

Glancing back at her, he forced a smile. *I love you.* Why was that so difficult to say? Was it because he wasn't sure of the truth of his words? These feelings roiling around inside of him were strange and unfamiliar. If it wasn't love, then it was probably insanity.

"Come on," he murmured. "Let's go to bed. The sooner this day ends, the better." He took her hand

and helped her to her feet, then followed her into his bedroom, his hands resting on her shoulders.

When they curled up beneath the covers, Eve fell asleep almost immediately. But Charlie was too restless to sleep. His mind was spinning, searching for a tiny bit of clarity.

He'd always prided himself on his ability to master any situation. There was that time he'd fallen into a crevice while climbing Mt. Rainier. And the avalanche he'd ridden down the side of a mountain in Utah while skiing. And the broken wrist he'd suffered three days into a wilderness hike in Arizona. He'd known exactly how to survive.

But this was different. Nothing in his life had prepared him for the onslaught of emotion, the highs and lows that seemed to toss him about like a rogue wave. His father had died before Charlie had really even recognized his parents' relationship. He should have learned about love from watching them.

Instead, he saw how his mother struggled, raising a family alone. She hadn't dated, hadn't even socialized with men after her husband's death. Charlie had once asked her why she hadn't tried to find someone else. She'd given him an odd look and said, "There was only one man for me," she'd said. "And for as long as I live, I will love him."

At the time, Charlie had idealized his mother's loyalty, made it into something much more than it was. But as he grew older, he saw how truly lonely she was. How much she missed the man she'd married. He could only imagine what they'd shared, only guess at the relationship they'd built together.

As an adult, Charlie never let himself feel that kind of loneliness. Instead, he consoled himself with an endless string of beautiful women, all of them willing to tell him what an incredible lover he was, what a great time they'd had.

Charlie rolled onto his side and stared at Evie's face. Her palms were pressed together and resting between the pillow and her cheek. This was the way she slept, all tidy and perfect. All the little things that he'd come to know about her—the expert technique she employed to peel an apple, the funny wrinkle in her nose when she brushed her teeth, the careful way she folded her bath towel.

Would these be the things he missed if he left? Charlie pushed up, swinging his legs off the edge of the bed. He wouldn't know unless he actually got away, took some time to put all of this in perspective.

"Oh, God," he murmured, rubbing his eyes with his fingertips. Making decisions used to be so much easier when he was on his own. Now, every decision seemed to be more crucial, filled with hidden twists and traps. Charlie grabbed a pair of jeans from a nearby chair and pulled them on, then tugged a T-shirt over his head.

He found his shoes under the sofa and his car keys

on the dining room table. Charlie grabbed a pen and scribbled a note to Eve, then took it back into the bedroom, laying it on his pillow.

He wasn't sure how much time he needed. Maybe a day. Maybe two. He had another presentation at the university on Tuesday. By then, he ought to know how he really felt. He'd either hop a plane for the job on Everest or ask Eve to move in with him permanently.

Charlie grabbed his jacket on the way back through the living room, then slipped out the front door into the predawn darkness. He had his cell phone. He'd text her later today and try to explain. Until then, he'd just see where the road took him.

EVE OPENED HER EYES, squinting to see the clock on the bedside table. Charlie's half of the bed was empty as usual. He was an early riser, even though he stayed up until she returned from the restaurant. He seemed to need so much less sleep than she did.

He usually got up shortly after dawn and took a long run, then had coffee at his favorite spot downtown, before walking home with the paper and a coffee for her. It had become a bit of a routine, changed daily by the kind of pastry he brought along with the coffee.

Eve pushed up on her elbow. It was nearly nine. He was usually back by now. She noticed the note on his pillow, then smiled. "Sweet," she murmured.

She grabbed the small piece of paper and rubbed her eyes before attempting to decipher his scrawl.

"I'm sorry. I had to go," she read. "Don't worry. I'll be back soon. Love you." Eve frowned. "Love you," she repeated. What was that supposed to mean? Had he just scribbled it as a quick end to his note? Or had he worried over the last line?

Eve shook her head. There was absolutely no reason to analyze the sentiment. The two words were merely a way of expressing affection. She crawled out of bed and wrapped the quilt around her body, then wandered out into the living room, searching for the smell of her morning coffee.

But to her surprise, Charlie wasn't there, in his usual spot on the sofa, the newspaper spread out in front of him. Eve frowned, then walked to the front door and pulled it open. He wasn't on the porch either.

An odd feeling settled in her stomach. His backpack was gone. His hiking boots, which usually sat beside the door, were also gone. She hurried to the kitchen, then looked out the window above the sink. The SUV was gone. She retrieved the note and reread it.

Wide-awake and with a few more facts to consider, Eve realized that the note could be read a different way. He wasn't just running out for coffee. Charlie was gone, the same way he'd left five years ago, only this time, he'd managed to leave a note.

Eve sat down on the edge of the bed and stared at his scrawl. She'd known this was coming. Sooner or later, he was bound to get restless. She drew a long breath, then let it out slowly, fighting back a sob. How long would he be gone this time? A month? A year?

Eve flopped back on the bed and put her arm over her eyes. No, he couldn't be gone for good, she thought to herself. He still had another lecture to do at the university. A sigh of relief slipped from her lips. He was just getting away for a while, taking a break. He just needed time to himself.

A knock sounded on the front door and a moment later, the bell rang. She found a pair of his jeans tossed over the end of the bed and pulled them on, then grabbed her shirt as she passed through the living room. A young man was standing on the opposite side of the door, an envelope in his hand.

"Hi," he said. "I'm from Dunbar Travel. Are you…" He paused and grinned. "You don't look like Charlie Templeton."

"I'm not. But he lives here."

"All right," he said. "Sign for these."

"What are they?" she asked, as she scribbled her name in his receipt book.

"Tickets," he said. "The itinerary is in the envelope."

She closed the door behind him, then crossed to the couch and sat down, tucking her feet beneath her. The envelope was open. If he was planning to surprise her with a trip, then she wanted to know so she could arrange her schedule. But there was another possibility—he was planning his escape.

Eve set the envelope down next to her as if it had burned her fingers. But after a minute of staring at it, she couldn't deny her curiosity any longer. She picked it up and pulled out the contents. "Denver to Boston," she murmured. She pulled out a second ticket. "Boston to London to New Delhi to Katmandu," she read. "Tickets for one."

He was due to leave at the end of next week. The flight to London was dated for a week after that. It didn't matter where he was now or whether he'd be back. In the end, Charlie was leaving the country again.

"YOU'RE HERE EARLY," Lily said. "Usually you don't get in before eleven. Not that I'm complaining. I'm glad you finally have a social life."

"Well, you'll be disappointed to know that it's all coming to an end. Charlie is gone."

"Gone?" Lily frowned. "Where?"

"I don't know. He just disappeared this morning. Said he'd be back soon. And then, some kid delivered plane tickets to his house. He's taking off in a week for…where is Katmandu? Morocco?"

"I think it's in Nepal," Lily said. "Or maybe Tibet?"

"Even worse," Eve said with a dry laugh. "That won't be an overnight trip." She strode to the sink and washed her hands, then grabbed an apron. A sharp knife and a big bowl of onions was all she really needed to work off her frustration.

Eve grabbed an onion and halved it, then peeled off the skin and began to chop it into tiny, even pieces. "I shouldn't be upset. I knew this was coming. I've been prepared. In fact, I'm glad he's leaving. It would be silly to invest any more time in a relationship that will never go anywhere."

Tears filled her eyes. She knew they weren't from the onions, but at least she had a cover while she gave in to her emotions. "He'll be back. And then we'll continue as we left off."

"But you want him to stay," Lily said.

"No!"

Lily nodded her head. "Yes."

"No," Eve insisted.

Lily gave her a pitying look. "Yes."

Eve brushed the tears from her cheeks with the back of her hand. "Yes," she finally murmured. "Of course I want him to stay. I have a man in my life and he's funny and kind and I think he genuinely cares about me. Why wouldn't I want that to continue?"

"Exactly," Lily said. "Just admit that you want a future with him. That's the first step."

"I admit it," Eve said. "Oh, God." She dropped the knife and sank onto a nearby stool. "This is going to end so badly." She grabbed a towel and wiped her runny nose, then looked at Lily through watery eyes. "I let myself fall in love with him."

"Not hard to do, considering how gorgeous he is."

"That's the point. I don't really even think about how he looks. He makes me laugh and he points out all my faults. He does things to my body that I never thought were possible. When we're together, we're... together. It's like we can't exist without touching or kissing or whispering." Eve took a ragged breath. "I do love him."

"So, tell him. Give him the choice. Love you or leave you."

"It's too soon," she said. "Nobody falls in love in just over a week."

"It hasn't been just a week. It's been five years."

"No," Eve said, shaking her head. But perhaps Lily was right. Maybe this feeling had begun all those years ago and had survived, buried somewhere in a quiet corner of her heart.

Lily stepped to her side. "There's nothing wrong with honesty," she said, grabbing the towel and dabbing at Eve's eyes. "Just tell him how you feel."

"I'll sound ridiculous," Eve said. "How can I feel this much in little more than a week?" She shook her head. "No. No! This is just an overreaction. It's because of the divorce. I'm making more of this than there really is. I did exactly the same thing with Matt after Charlie left. I made him into some white knight. I'm not going to do that again."

"All right. Then dump him. Dump Charlie. That will make you feel better, won't it? Get him out of your life for good. Put this all behind you and move on."

"I will," Eve said. "As soon as I figure out where he is. Or when he's coming back."

He'd taken all his camping gear. She knew one place where he might be. When they'd gone camping together, he'd mentioned that he'd stayed at that site many times. It was close by and not a difficult hike. Tomorrow, she'd hike up there and tell him how she felt.

And in between now and then, she'd try her very best to figure out how she felt.

CHARLIE WINCED as he removed his hiking boot. It had been a stupid accident, one that was easily preventable had he been paying attention to the trail ahead. But his mind had been occupied with thoughts of Eve.

He'd been out in the woods for a day, hoping that fresh air and solitude would clear his mind and make his decisions easier. One misplaced footstep and he'd gone down, his ankle rolling to the side.

By the time he'd removed his sock, the ankle had already begun to swell. "Not good," he muttered. His cell phone was back at camp, but he was almost certain he'd get no signal. The only choice he had was to wait, let the swelling go down and walk out.

Charlie wiggled his toes, then tested the motion of his foot. He was pretty certain it wasn't broken. Balancing himself on a nearby tree, he stood and tried to put weight on it, then hobbled a few feet down the trail and back. He wouldn't be able to go far, at least not for a day or two. But he had enough food to last a week. Though the river was a complicated trip on one foot, he could easily slide down on his ass and climb up on his knees.

Like any good outdoorsman, Charlie began to formulate a plan. He was only about a hundred yards from his campsite. First, he needed to cut down the swelling. The river would be icy cold from the runoff in the mountains. He'd go soak his ankle, then crawl back up to his campsite before dark. If he elevated it overnight, he might be able to walk out tomorrow.

Charlie searched around in the underbrush for a sturdy stick. He found one dangling from a nearby sapling and pulled down. It wasn't the best, but it had a nice joint to tuck under his arm. He pulled off his T-shirt and wrapped it around the Y in the branch, then gave it a test. Though it was a bit long, he could take care of that problem with his hatchet.

As he struggled back toward his campsite, he couldn't help but think about how this little accident had completely taken his mind off Eve.

He'd thought solitude would clear his mind. But

instead, he'd spent most of his time thinking about their last trip together, the seduction in the cold night, lying next to the campfire. The feel of her naked body curled up against his. The pleasure of waking up to the sounds of the trees rustling outside and the soft rhythm of her breathing.

He'd planned to spend just one more night in the woods before heading back to Boulder. The day after tomorrow, he was due at the university for another lecture and he had every intention of keeping that appointment. If he couldn't hike out under his own power, they'd come looking for him. And Eve could guess where he might have gone.

By the time he'd made it down to the river, Charlie's ankle was throbbing from the pain. He sat down on a boulder, then slid over to the edge of the water, plunging his foot into the rushing current.

"Shit," he muttered, wincing at the icy cold. He closed his eyes, then waited as long as he could before he took his foot out. Though it felt considerably better, it didn't look much different.

"Charlie!"

He straightened at the sound of his name, looking up along the bank toward the woods. "Yeah?"

"Charlie? Where are you?"

"Eve? I'm down here. At the river."

A few seconds later, she emerged from the woods, her hair tangled and her face dirty. She stumbled up to his side and threw herself into his arms. "Oh, God. You're safe. You're alive."

He stared at her in disbelief. "What the hell are you doing here?"

"I found your daypack on the trail and it was all torn apart. I thought you'd been eaten by a bear. Or a wolf. Or a cougar." She held his face in her hands. "Are you sure you're all right? Why did you leave your pack there?"

"I twisted my ankle," he said, then stopped. "I didn't leave it behind all that long ago." He craned his neck to scan the woods. "A bear might have gotten at it. Or a very determined squirrel. Damn it, Eve, you shouldn't be hiking alone. Never, ever, hike alone."

"I could have been eaten by a bear?" she said.

"He probably wouldn't have eaten you." He shrugged. "Well, not unless you ran into a grizzly. Black bears usually run when they see humans. But—that's not the point. Never hike alone."

"You're hiking alone," she said.

"I have a little bit of experience in the woods," he replied. "And look what happened to me."

She took a ragged breath. "I had to find you. We need to talk."

"Right now?"

"No, not this minute." She glanced down at his foot. "What happened? Your ankle is all swollen."

"I sprained my ankle. I told you. That's why I left my pack on the trail. Are you all right? Did you hit your head?" She seemed completely flustered, as if her time alone in the woods had unhinged her a bit. This was not the calm and organized Eve he knew and loved.

"It's a little scary out here all alone," she said, glancing around. "I wasn't sure I knew my way. I had my cell phone along, just in case, but—"

"Your cell phone won't work out here," he said.

"It worked earlier. I called Lily at the restaurant to tell her about the new blender I ordered and she said…"

"Your phone worked?"

She nodded, then held it out to him. He turned it on, but there was no signal. "It doesn't work now. How long ago did it work?"

"A half-hour," she said, glancing at her watch. "I called her at two-thirty. It's quarter after three now."

"Two miles," he murmured. "Maybe three. So, what was so important that you braved the wilds to find me?"

She gave him an odd look, opening her mouth, then snapping it shut. "Nothing," she finally murmured. "It seemed important at the time, but it's not. We can talk about it later." She pointed to his foot. "Doesn't that hurt?"

Charlie nodded. "Yeah. It's a pretty bad sprain. I don't think it's broken, though."

"How were you going to walk on it?"

"I wasn't," Charlie said. "I was going to give it a few days, see if it felt better. I figured if I missed my lecture, someone would come looking and rescue me. And here you are."

"I can't carry you out," she said. "You're too heavy."

"If you can get cell phone service an hour down the trail, then we can walk to that point and call."

"You can't walk," she said.

"It will be a little slow going. It shouldn't take us longer than three or four hours." He stood, but the moment he put even a tiny bit of weight on his ankle the pain was unbearable.

"You'll never be able to walk on it. I ran into some mountain bikers on the trail," she said, glancing between his foot and his face. "Maybe if we yell, they'll hear us."

"I don't think yelling is going to help," he said.

She chewed on her lower lip for a long moment, then took a deep breath and stood. "I'll go. If I hurry, I can bring back help right away." She sat back down. "I don't want to go. What if I run into a bear? It was stupid of me to come out here alone."

He reached out and put his arm around her. "Then you'll stay. Maybe tomorrow, my ankle will feel good enough for both of us to walk out. Come on, help me back up to the camp and I'll make us some dinner."

Charlie had no idea what had brought Eve to the woods, but it must have been something pretty important. He thought about pressing her further, but then decided that they had the entire night together. Sooner or later, she'd tell him.

When they got back the campsite, Eve perched on the log next to the fire, watching him warily. "I was surprised when I woke up yesterday and you were gone."

"I left the note," Charlie said.

"I thought you were gone for good. Like the last time."

"Eve, you knew I had to be back for my lecture. Besides, I said in my note that I'd be back." He sighed, then sat down beside her. "I'd never leave without saying goodbye. Not this time."

"And what has changed?" she asked.

"A lot. My feelings for you...they're different. Deeper. More...durable."

"And you think they're strong enough to last over another long separation? Another five years?"

"I'm not going away for five years," Charlie reassured her.

"But you are going away," she said. Eve reached into her jacket pocket, then held out an envelope. "These are for you. They were delivered yesterday morning. I signed for them."

"Them?"

"They're airline tickets. For your trip to Katmandu." She paused. "You could have told me you were planning to leave."

"I wasn't," he said. "I hadn't made a decision."

"Plane tickets aren't a decision?" She held up her hand. "I'm not angry. We knew this time would come. You need to go back to your life and I need to go back to mine. Besides, I'm not going to be here anyway. I—I'm going to open my restaurant in Seattle. I have investors and they've found a good location. I should have—"

He stopped her words with his finger, pressing it against her lips. "How do you really feel, Eve? Say it. Out loud. Tell me what you want."

He saw the indecision in her face. She still didn't trust him. Hell, if he could turn back time, he'd do it in a heartbeat. His choice to leave her the first time had been the worst decision in his life and now he was paying for it. But he couldn't force her to trust him. He'd have to show her that he planned to stick around.

"I'm not going to Katmandu," he said. "I'm not taking the job. The guy who found the job for me just assumed I'd be anxious to go. He was wrong." Charlie chuckled. "Besides, if this ankle is broken, I'm not going to climb Everest in a month."

"What kind of job is it?" she asked.

"It's a television special for National Geographic about the ecological and social impact of the climbing business on Everest."

"It sounds important," she said.

"It is, kind of," Charlie admitted. "I'm really not

sure I could do it. I write. But with this, I'd be on camera a lot."

"Oh, you'd be great," Eve said. "You'd be perfect."

"You think so?"

She nodded. "Charlie, you have to do it. It's about ecology. It's your moral duty to do it. Don't you want to stand up for a cause that's important?"

"Of course I do. But it's going to take me away from you."

"We haven't made any promises to each other. You should go." She drew in a deep breath, then smiled. "You should." Eve got to her feet, then brushed off her backside. "I'm going to walk down the trail and see if I can get cell phone service. Maybe I'll run into those mountain bikers and they can help."

He considered her offer for a long moment, then shook his head. "No, I don't want you out there alone. Stay here with me. Help will come."

"I'll be back in a little while," she said.

He didn't want her to leave, but she seemed determined to put some distance between them, no matter what the cost. And when Eve made a decision, she usually couldn't be swayed. "Be careful," he said.

"I will."

"If you're not back here in an hour, I'm coming to look for you."

She leaned over and gave him a quick kiss. But Charlie grabbed her and pulled her into his embrace, his balance wavering for a moment. His lips found hers and he kissed her, deeply and thoroughly. And when she was nearly breathless from the experience, he drew back.

"I love you, Evie."

She looked up at him, her eyes wide. For a moment, he thought she might return the sentiment. Instead, she just blinked. "I should go."

Charlie nodded. Whether she believed him or not didn't matter. He'd told her how he felt. And he'd certainly showed her how he felt. Now, she'd have to figure out what to make of it.

He watched her walk out of camp. "Make a lot of noise while you're walking," he called. "Sing."

The sound of her voice drifted back to him. "What should I sing?" she called. A few moments later, the strains of "My Country 'Tis of Thee" came through the trees.

"Oh, Evie, I do love you," he murmured. "And I'm pretty sure you love me." Now if he could just get her to admit it, they could start planning a future together.

7

EVE SAT QUIETLY ON A BENCH in the ranger station, the quiet pace belying the fact that a rescue operation was underway. Any moment now, Charlie would return to the station, rescued by two men driving ATVs.

She met up with a group of eight mountain bikers fifteen minutes down the trail. Half the group had walked with her until she could get cell phone service and the other half had set off for Charlie's campsite.

In the end, she'd been ordered to wait on the trail until the rangers arrived. One had returned her to the station while the other two had gone on to get Charlie and his gear.

"Don't worry. Your husband will be fine."

Eve looked up to find a female ranger standing in front of her, a clipboard in her hands. "He's not my husband," she said.

"Well, he will still be fine. We handle all sorts of emergencies here. And lots of sprained ankles and broken legs. People seem to get particularly clumsy walking through the woods." She sat down next to Eve. "Can I get you anything?"

"Sure. Do you have a psychiatrist handy? Because I really need to talk to someone." The ranger gave Eve an odd look, then slowly stood. "I'm kidding," Eve said. "I just heard something out there in the woods that I never thought I'd hear. And I'm not sure how to take it."

"This isn't one of those alien stories, is it?" the ranger asked. "Because we get a lot of those, too."

"No," Eve insisted. "No, I'm not crazy. My boyfriend just blurted out that he loved me and I'm not sure what to think about that. We've only been together two weeks. Well, we were together for a month and two weeks five years ago. Or five years and two weeks. Don't you think that's kind of soon to be saying something like that?"

Eve wasn't sure why she was unburdening herself to a complete stranger. Maybe she wanted a totally unbiased opinion. Lily would never give it to her. And if she asked her mother, that would set off a firestorm of wedding plans that Eve wasn't prepared to deal with.

"I guess he wouldn't say it if he didn't mean it," the ranger said.

"But maybe it was just one of those casual 'I love

yous.' You know the kind. Love you, babe. Men toss those off all the time and it doesn't mean they want to settle down and have children with you. My ex-husband told me that he loved me and he didn't."

"I think you might be overanalyzing this," the ranger said.

"What is your name? I mean, your first name. Your badge says 'Beckham'."

"Carly," the ranger said.

"Carly, have you ever met a guy and been so incredibly attracted to him you can't think straight?"

"Sure," Carly said. "I love when that happens. Although it doesn't happen that often. A few years back, there was this ranger who started working here and he was gorgeous. His name was Eric. Ranger Eric. I mean, I usually have my pick of guys. Look at me, I'm the only woman at this location. But this guy was so amazing. And he knew it. We dated for a month and then he informed me he was being transferred to a post in Wyoming. He knew this when we started sleeping together but he didn't think it was important enough to tell me."

"That's exactly what happened to me. Charlie just disappeared one day. He didn't even tell me he was leaving. These guys are…drifters. You know in your heart they're bad for you, but you can't help yourself. He was gone for five years and then one day he just showed up again. Like he'd never been gone at all."

"And now he loves you?" Carly asks.

"That's what he says. I'm not sure I should believe him."

"Maybe it's just taken him five years to figure it out. Sometimes men can be so slow at those things."

The door to the ranger station opened and Carly stood up. Eve waited, then smiled as Charlie hobbled in with a pair of crutches.

"That's him?" Carly asked.

Eve nodded.

"Oh, girl, if a man like that told me he loved me, I'd put all my doubts aside and marry him as soon as possible." She pressed her hand to her heart. "Goodness, he is gorgeous."

But Ranger Carly's words didn't soothe Eve's doubts. Matt had been a pretty ordinary guy and he'd fallen prey to other women. How was she supposed to keep a guy like Charlie interested—especially for the rest of her life? What was it that attracted him to her—besides her skills in the kitchen?

Maybe she'd have to resort to cooking meat, Eve mused. If he couldn't get it at home, then he'd go other places to find it—fast food restaurants filled with pretty young women, butcher shops filled with pretty young women, steakhouses…filled with pretty young women.

"Hey. You made it back," Charlie said, crossing the room to stand in front of her.

"No bears," Eve said. "It wasn't so bad. I ran into the bikers soon after I left you. And all I saw on the trail were a few squirrels and a very big crow."

"Come on. They're going to take us to get our cars and then I have to stop by a hospital and get an X-ray." He pulled her into a hug. "Thanks for rescuing me, Evie. I don't know what I would have done without you."

"I'm sure you would have survived. You don't need me."

He drew back, frowning at her. His hand cupped her cheek and he ran his thumb over her lips. "Where would you get an idea like that? Of course I need you." He kissed her softly, then grinned. "Come on. I'm ready to get out of the woods and find a nice soft spot to rest my ankle." He leaned closer to whisper in her ear. "My bed, preferably, with you in it."

As she walked out of the ranger station, Carly gave her a thumbs-up. Eve smiled weakly. Everyone else seemed to be convinced Charlie was the perfect man for her. Now, she just had to convince herself.

CHARLIE STRETCHED OUT on the leather couch in his living room, his ankle propped up on a pillow. Eve was in the kitchen, making them both lunch while he watched a Rockies game on television.

He smiled to himself. Since they'd returned from the woods yesterday, he and Eve had settled back into their life together. She'd decided to take the day off from the restaurant to work on her cookbook, testing recipes in his kitchen. She claimed using his kitchen was better since it contained consumer appliances, which her readers would be using anyway.

Charlie preferred to think she just wanted to spend more time with him. After discovering his plans to go back to Nepal, she'd begun to see their time together as finite. Charlie hadn't bothered to tell her he had decided not to take the job.

The way he figured, it would be a good test, a chance to find out how she really felt. As the time grew closer for him to "leave," her true feelings would be revealed. And if she asked him to stay, or begged him to stay as he imagined it, then he'd know they had a future together.

Though it wasn't the best way to go about gauging her feelings, it was the only option open to him. Every time he tried to discuss the future, Eve quickly changed the subject. It wasn't difficult for him to understand her reluctance, especially after her divorce.

But it was more than just a general distrust of men, Charlie mused. He suspected she was afraid her career would suffer if she committed to a relationship. Over the past week, she'd spent very little time at the restaurant and he could see how torn she was about it. The only factor that saved her was her belief he'd be gone in a week or two and her life would return to normal.

Charlie grabbed his crutches and hopped up on one foot. He made his way to the kitchen, standing in the doorway and watching her as she bent over the counter, her back toward him. "How's it going?"

Eve glanced over her shoulder. "Really well," she said. "Here, come and taste." She moved to the stove, then stirred a pot, before scooping out a ladle of soup into a bowl. "I love soup," she said with a sigh. "It's the perfect food."

"I always thought hot dogs were the perfect food," Charlie said.

She groaned. "Have I taught you nothing?"

"It's a meal in a bun. Tacos are almost as good, but they're a lot messier. Anything wrapped in anything else is my idea of a perfect meal. You can put it in your pocket, eat it in the car, and not have to bother with a fork and a knife."

"Taste it," she said.

"Tofu?" he asked.

Eve shook her head. "It's a five-bean chili with TVP instead of meat. There are seven different vegetables in it."

Charlie gave it a taste and smiled. "It's good. It's really good. It's kind of sweet and smoky."

"Molasses," she said. "And Dijon mustard. I think it's just about right. Spicy, but not too spicy."

"Man, if you could dehydrate this, I know a lot of climbers who'd eat this every night for dinner."

"It would taste pretty good dehydrated," she said. "The beans would hold up really well."

He leaned back on the counter. "We should start a business together," he said. "There's a good-sized market for dehydrated foods. Especially foods that taste good and pack a lot of calories and carbs into a small amount of space. Campers and climbers would love it—and probably the military, too. Astronauts. There's another market, although it's a small niche."

Eve giggled. But then her smile faded slightly. "You really think there's a market?"

"I know a lot of climbers who are vegetarian. And those who aren't would buy this just because it tasted so good."

"I have a dehydrator at the restaurant. I use it for fresh herbs and fruit. We'd have to cook all the ingredients separately. You couldn't just dump soup into it and expect it to work."

"I know a guy who runs an outfitting company and he's always looking for new ventures. He'd carry this, I'm sure of it. And a lot of the expeditions on Everest use him for their equipment and supplies."

"I have a lot of other recipes that would work," Eve said, excitement growing in her voice. "We could—" She stopped suddenly. "I could—"

"No," Charlie said. "*We.* We could do this together." He reached over and touched her arm. "I'm thinking I might stick around awhile. I can't do this forever. I mean, living out of a backpack, sleeping in a tent. Maybe it's time to get on with the rest of my life."

"No," she said.

"No?" He frowned. "No to the business? Or no to the sticking around?"

"We had an agreement," she said.

Charlie laughed. "We never had any agreement. Did I sign something I wasn't aware of? I mean, there have been times over the past two weeks when I've lost touch with reality, mostly when we're in bed." He cleared his throat. "No, always when we're in bed. Unless I signed your agreement then, I don't remember."

"You know what I mean," Eve said. "You're supposed to go away again. And I'm supposed to carry on with my life. That's the way I had it planned."

"Well, plans change," he said, his tone sharp with anger. Frustration welled up inside of him. This was crazy. He was in love with Eve Keller and she refused to believe him. Maybe this was just all poetic justice. He'd seduced so many women that he'd lost all credibility.

"Please, don't do this," Eve said.

"How do you feel?" Charlie asked, grabbing her arms and turning her to face him. He touched her head. "Not in here, but in here." He pressed his palm to her chest. "I know how I feel, Eve. I'm falling in love with you. Hell, I might as well admit it. I *am* in love with you. And I understand why you might not believe me, but you're going to have to trust me on this."

"Why? So you can reassure yourself you're just a normal guy with normal needs? What's to stop you from changing your mind? Millions of guys do it. Just because you love me now doesn't mean you'll love me in a year or two."

"You're right," he said. "But sometimes you just have to go on faith. You have to take a chance and see the possibilities." He leaned close and touched his lips to hers. "You can't deny there's something incredible between us."

"Sex isn't love," she said. "And desire isn't fidelity. I'm not stupid enough to believe that."

"So, I'm paying for the mistakes you made with your ex?"

"Mistakes *I* made? He was the one who cheated."

"You were the one who married him."

She cursed softly, slamming the spoon down on the counter. "Don't you dare blame all of that on me. You share just as much of the blame."

"All right," Charlie said. "Now we're getting somewhere. Yes, I will take part of the blame. I was an idiot to leave you. I should never have walked out. I made the biggest mistake of my life and now, I'm paying for it."

She opened her mouth as if to snap back at him,

but then her expression softened. "Only some mistakes can't be fixed. No matter how hard you want to try," she said in a defeated tone. Eve took a ragged breath. "I should go. I have to work. I've stayed away from the restaurant for far too long."

"No, we're going to settle this. Right here and right now," Charlie said. "I want to know where I stand."

She closed her eyes and shook her head. "I can't make any promises," Eve murmured. "I won't. Not now."

"So you want me to leave?"

"Of course not," she said.

"You want me to stay?"

"You have to work. And you have a chance to do that in Nepal. I'm not going to keep you from leaving. And I'm not going to ask you to stay. Make up your own mind."

With that, she turned and strode out of the kitchen. Charlie heard the front door slam and he cursed out loud. What had ever made him believe this would be easy? He'd always thought if he found the right woman, everything would work out like it was supposed to. But now, he felt as if he was in the middle of a battle of wills—and he was losing.

What more was he supposed to do to prove his feelings to her? He limped over to the kitchen table and sat down. Eve had made cornbread and the loaf was cooling in front of him. He took a knife and cut off a huge slice, then slowly bit into it.

"Oh, God," he murmured. Charlie reached for the butter and slathered a good measure on the warm bread. There were so many things he loved about Eve. The way her naked body felt against his, the taste of her mouth when he kissed her, the scent of her damp hair after a shower. Now he could add her cornbread and five-bean chili to his list.

"THEY WANT US TO FLY TO Seattle this weekend. All the investors are going to be in town and they'd like you to cook for them on Sunday night."

"This weekend?" Eve sighed. After two days off, she'd put in a long night in the kitchen, a night filled with confusion over Charlie. The last thing she wanted to talk about was business. "I'm not ready. I need time to plan a menu."

"Cook what you cook at the restaurant every day," Lily said. "That's what they're looking for. They've got a restaurant booked and you can use their kitchen. You're supposed to call with a list of supplies you'll need. And we'll shop when we get out there." She paused. "And they want you to do at least a few seafood dishes."

"Why? They know I'm a vegetarian chef."

"They think the restaurant would be more popular if you at least had three or four fish and seafood dishes on the menu. It works for us here. And Seattle is a fish town."

Eve shook her head. "If they really want me, then

they'll take me the way I am." Though Eve wanted to sound as if she were standing on principle, she knew that her argument had nothing to do with her beliefs as a cook. She wanted to spend every last day she could with Charlie.

"Eve, you can convince them of that *after* you cook for them," Lily said. "Just give them a chance to get to know you."

"The Garden Gate is about vegetarian cuisine. Our decision to serve fish and seafood was out of financial necessity. We always said we'd go back to strict vegetarian as soon as business was good. It's been good for a couple years now and I say it's time to change back."

"What is wrong with you? I thought this was what you wanted," Lily said. "These investors are interested in you. They believe in you."

Eve sat down on a kitchen stool and buried her face in her hands. "I'm sorry," she mumbled. "I'm just really tired. I haven't been sleeping much."

"Maybe if you came home and slept in your own bed, you wouldn't be so tired."

"It's not because I've been having nonstop sex," Eve explained. "Well, I actually have, but that's not why I'm tired."

"Would you care to share? Or am I supposed to guess?" Lily said after a long silence.

"Charlie is talking about staying in Boulder. Indefinitely. In fact, he made a business proposal to me earlier today. And it's actually something pretty intriguing." She shook her head. "I don't know why I'm even considering these feelings I have."

"Maybe because you'd like to believe there is a man out there who is absolutely perfect for you? And that man is Charlie?"

"How am I supposed to know?"

"Well, maybe you can't," Lily said. "Not after just a week or two. You need more time."

"He seems to know exactly how he feels."

Lily held up her hand. "Wait a second. This sounds like a discussion that would be best paired with a nice pinot noir."

"Make it a cabernet," Eve said. "The good stuff. That Whitehill reserve. And bring the whole bottle."

Lily disappeared into the dining room and a few seconds later returned empty-handed.

"What? We can't be out of Whitehill," Eve said. "We had a whole case last week."

"You have a visitor," Lily said.

"Charlie?"

Lily shook her head. "Matt. He said it's important. He said he'll only take a few minutes of your time."

"I don't want to talk to him," Eve said. "Tell him he can call my lawyer if he has anything to say."

"I don't think he'll leave unless you talk to him," Lily said.

Eve stood up, shoving the stool back across the tile floor. She stalked out of the kitchen, the door swinging closed behind her. Glancing back, she saw Lily peering out of the small window and she waved her off. When Eve reached the bar area, she found Matt sitting alone, nursing a beer.

Eve met Kenny's gaze and smiled at the bartender. "Can you give us a few minutes?" she asked. "Maybe you could start going through the wine order and get that ready for tomorrow?"

"Sure, boss," Kenny said. He wiped his wet hands on a towel, then walked back to the kitchen.

"What do you want?"

Matt looked up at her and pasted a weak smile on his face. "Hello, Eve."

She pointed a finger at him. "I'm not going to discuss the divorce settlement with you. Talk to my lawyer."

"That's not what this is about." He pointed to the stool next to his. "Sit. I just have to say a few things and then, if you like, I'll get out of your life for good."

He seemed so defeated, his usual arrogance completely drained. Curious, Eve sat down, leaving a single barstool as a buffer between them. "Go ahead."

"I want you to know that I love you, Eve."

Eve jumped up. "What is this? Is there something in the water? Suddenly, everyone loves me. I've been hearing it all day long. Just a few weeks ago, I was wondering if I'd ever be with anyone ever again. Now men are falling at my feet."

"Men?"

"Yes," Eve said sarcastically. "Men. Hundreds of them."

"I guess I can see why," Matt murmured. "They can see what I was too stupid to notice. What a great woman you are."

"Oh, please. Just tell me how much money you want and get it over with. I have a bottle of wine to drink and a cheesecake to eat."

"I—I didn't come here for money."

"That's not what you were saying the last time we talked. You were ready to renegotiate the divorce settlement."

"I just came to see—I mean, I was hoping you'd— I wanted to let you know that if there was any chance for us, you know, to fix the past—to get back together and try again—then I'd like to do that."

Eve couldn't believe what she was hearing. "No, there's no chance of that. Why would you even ask?"

"I just wanted to make sure," Matt said. "Cause I'm—I guess I'm getting married again."

"All right," Eve said, standing up and pressing her palms on the bar. "This is just too weird. You need to leave."

"No, it's true," Matt said. "This girl I've been dating just told me she's pregnant. And the baby is mine.

When she told me, I kind of freaked out. I mean, it's a lot to take in. And the expense is…" His voice trailed off. "Now that it's really over with us, I guess I'm going to marry her instead."

"So she's getting you by default?" Eve slowly sat back down. "Matt, listen to me. Listen very carefully. If you don't love her, then don't pretend you do. Don't make her believe something that isn't true. Work hard and give her money to help raise your child, be a good father, but don't make her think you'll ever love her if you won't."

"You don't think I could love her?"

"Men don't change. She might not know about all the things that messed up our marriage and maybe that won't make a difference, but—"

"Actually, she does," Matt said. "I kind of dated her while we were married. And then, a few months ago, we hooked up again and one thing led to another and here I am. About to become a dad." His hand shook as he picked up his beer glass. He took a long swallow. "I don't know what to do. I think I really screwed up this time."

"You really want my advice?" Eve asked.

"I do," he replied.

"Be a man," she said softly. Even after all this time and all that had passed between them, she felt a bit sorry for Matt. She felt a whole lot worse for the woman who was carrying his child and for the child itself, who'd grow up with a jerk for a father. Still, there was no reason to make him feel worse than he already did. "You can change. You can be the best father ever."

"No," he murmured.

She reached out and covered his hand with hers. "You can. It'll be hard work and sometimes you'll want to walk away. But you're going to be a father and raising this child is going to be the most important thing you ever do in your life. You need to do it right."

He smiled wanly. "My dad was never around. And when he was, he and my mom were always fighting. I used to tell myself I'd do a much better job once I became a father."

"Then prove it," Eve said.

"You really think I can change?" he asked, his expression filled with disbelief.

"Absolutely," Eve said. Though it might have been the biggest lie she ever told in her life, Eve knew she'd done the right thing.

Her words seemed to give him courage. He drained the rest of his glass, then stood up. "I can. I'm going to go talk to her right now. Get this all figured out. And when that baby comes, I'm going to be a good dad."

She watched him walk out the front door. He turned and waved at her and Eve sent him an encouraging smile. When he was gone, she walked to the end of the bar and pulled a bottle of the reserve Cabernet from the tall wooden wine rack.

She quickly opened it and poured a glass, then sat down at the bar and took a sip. Eve couldn't help but wonder why she'd encouraged Matt. Did she really believe a man could change?

Throughout her parents' marriage, her father had never changed. Eve wasn't sure he'd ever wanted to. He enjoyed his life exactly the way it was, with all the petty dramas and imagined passions. Her mother had chosen to put up with it—and still did for all Eve knew.

But when those same problems had haunted her own marriage, Eve had stood up and taken a stand. It wasn't out of courage that she'd walked away from her first marriage. It was out of fear. Fear that she'd become her mother—a woman who was willing to put her own emotions aside just to keep her marriage intact.

Maybe that's why Eve worked so hard at her career. She'd never have to depend upon a man to take care of her, to be the center of her life. If she was going to love a man, and trust him with her whole soul, he had to be someone who could tolerate her independent streak.

Was Charlie that man? "Probably," Eve murmured. He liked her exactly the way she was.

In the short time they'd been together again, Eve had been forced to admit that he was different from the man she'd known five years ago. And she was a different woman. But was she willing to risk her heart one more time? Did she have the strength to stick with it, to weather the bad times without bailing yet again?

Maybe she could have made her marriage to Matt work. She hadn't really tried to save it once she found out about his cheating. They might have been happy, had he agreed to give up the other women. But Eve doubted they ever would have found the kind of passion she shared with Charlie. It just hadn't been there with Matt.

It just wasn't in her nature to trust easily. She wanted to love Charlie, or at least believe that love was possible. And yet, she knew the more time she invested in him, the harder it would be to let him go. She already felt something deeper for him than she'd ever felt for another man. And they'd been together two weeks.

"Are you all right?"

The sound of Lily's voice startled her and Eve turned as her friend sat down beside her. "Yes," she murmured, forcing a smile. "I'm fine."

"What did he want?"

"He wanted to tell me he's going to be a father," Eve said.

"Matt?"

"Yes," Eve said. She sighed softly. "And I wished

him well." Pushing away from the bar, Eve stood. "I have to go. Can you close up for me?"

"Sure. Listen, why don't we just leave everything for tomorrow morning? We'll go get a drink somewhere. Have some fun."

"I have something to do," Eve said. "Maybe another time." She slipped out of her chef's coat and draped it over the back of a stool, then gave Lily a clumsy hug.

"What is it?" Lily asked, staring at Eve's somber expression.

"I think I might be in love." Eve drew a ragged breath. "Or maybe I am in love. I'm not sure. But I have to figure out what to do about it." She grabbed the open bottle of wine and walked out the front door.

8

THE NIGHT WAS SILENT all around him. In the distance the sound of a car horn could be heard and then, silence again. Charlie sat on the porch of his house, a beer in his hand, his feet kicked up on the railing.

He used to love the silence of the outdoors—a thick forest, a desolate mountaintop, a remote beach. No human sounds except for the gentle rhythm of his breathing.

But that had changed. Now, he craved the sound of her voice, her laugh, her footsteps on his front porch. Charlie loved the way she hummed in the morning while making coffee for him or the awful songs she sang in the shower. With every sound Eve made, it reminded him that she was his—at least for the moment.

Since their argument earlier in the day, Charlie had considered calling her at least once every five minutes. But he'd decided to wait, to see if she followed form and showed up at his house after work. He glanced at his watch. She was already an hour overdue.

He cursed softly, then swung his legs down from the railing. If he wasn't so determined to force her to make the next move, he'd go down to the restaurant, walk into her kitchen and kiss some sense into her. What was she so damned afraid of?

Maybe things wouldn't work out between them. Maybe they were just fooling themselves. But they wouldn't know unless they tried and she was too scared to even make an attempt. Either her marriage must have done a real number on her confidence or there was something else at work here.

He stood and walked over to the porch swing. His ankle was still a bit sore but on the mend. The doctor had diagnosed a bad sprain, but could find no permanent damage. Though Charlie had been searching for reasons not to go to Nepal, his ankle wouldn't be one of them.

He stretched out on the cushioned seat and closed his eyes, letting images of Eve drift through his mind. Though they'd been physically intimate from the start, they still didn't know each other emotionally. He could tell by the look in her eyes how she was feeling at any given moment. But he couldn't always tell why.

They hadn't spent much of their time talking about

their pasts. He didn't know much about her family, only that her parents lived in Arizona, her father loved to golf, her mother taught her to cook, and she was an only child. That wasn't much—not for two people who loved each other.

He already knew she loved clover honey in her chamomile tea and that she preferred pinot noir over merlot. That she loved every kind of bean except lima beans. That the only thing she wanted after a long day of work was a foot massage. That was a helluva lot more than he knew about her five years ago.

The sound of footsteps on the front walk caught his attention and he held his breath. A moment later, Charlie saw her standing in front of the door. She reached out to knock, then decided to grab the key from its spot behind the mailbox.

"It's unlocked," he said.

She jumped at the sound of his voice, spinning around to face him. "You scared me!"

Charlie pushed to his feet. "Sorry." Slowly, he approached her, trying to read her expression in the feeble light from the street lamps. "Sorry," he repeated. "I am sorry."

"I know. You said that."

"I meant for earlier. The fight we had. I'm sorry."

"It wasn't a fight," Eve said. "More like a disagreement. We can't possibly get along every moment of every day, can we?"

Charlie shook his head and took another step closer. One more step and their bodies touched. He reached down and slipped his arm around her waist, pulling her close. He brushed his lips over hers in a teasing, fleeting kiss, daring her to ask for more. But she just stared up into his eyes.

"Are you going to Nepal?" she asked.

"Not right this minute," he replied with a grin.

"Are you going next week?"

Charlie knew the job was something he ought to take. And at any other time in his life, he would have jumped at it. So why was he waffling now? Because he finally had a reason to stay in one place for a while—and that reason was standing right in front of him. "Do you want me to go?"

Eve hesitated for a moment, then nodded. "I think it's a wonderful opportunity. And when either of us has a wonderful opportunity, we should take it. We were apart for five years and look at what happened when we got back together. I think we could probably stand to be apart for a few months."

Charlie studied her for a long moment. She was absolutely right. Though he wanted her to beg him to stay, he knew it wasn't in her nature to make demands on him. Maybe that was part of why he loved her—because she didn't force him to be anyone but himself. "You're right. The job is too good to turn down." He paused. "I should go to Nepal," Charlie said. "Next week. But right now, I'm going to bed."

He stepped away from her and walked to the door. "Are you coming?" She hesitated for a few seconds, then followed him. Charlie took her hand and drew her inside.

The moment the door closed, they began to shed their clothes, tossing them on the floor at their feet. They were naked before they got through the living room and Charlie pressed her back against the wall, her body warm against his.

He searched her mouth for some reassurance that their argument had been forgotten, but he didn't find it there. Instead, he found it in her response to his caress. He slid down her body, finding her nipple and drawing it to a peak with his tongue. She moaned softly and he felt her surrender, her body going soft and pliant beneath his touch.

He moved back up to kiss her again, his fingers slipping between her legs and gently teasing at her desire. She reached out to touch him but the moment she did, Charlie had to stop her. He was so close to the edge already. One perfect caress might send him over.

Yet she wouldn't be denied the pleasure of touching him. She began slowly, knowing exactly how to delay his release. They knew each other's bodies so well already. But Charlie wanted more.

When he felt her rising toward her orgasm, he picked her up and wrapped her legs around his waist. A stab of pain shot up his leg from his sore ankle, but

Charlie ignored it, focusing on the exquisite anticipation of their joining.

He drew her down on his shaft in one smooth motion. It happened so quickly, so easily, that she gasped in surprise. And then, as if she couldn't help herself, Eve dissolved into the sweet spasms of her orgasm.

Though Charlie tried to hold back, the sound of her moans made it impossible. He drew back, then drove into her, pressing her against the wall, his hands clutching at her backside. Wave after wave of pleasure washed over him as he lost himself in the heat of her body. His legs suddenly went weak and his ankle began to throb. It was all he could do to keep them both upright.

When the sensations finally subsided, he carried her into his bedroom and gently laid her on the bed, bracing himself above her. He was still hard and he teased her a bit more, slowly sliding in and out of her. At first, she wriggled beneath him, trying to stop him. But then, gradually, he felt her reactions change.

This time Charlie didn't rush. Instead, they played at lovemaking for a long time. The frantic connection they made against the wall had been purely for physical release. But this was for something more than raw desire. This was affection and trust. And love.

When he brought her to completion again, Charlie

kissed her as she tumbled over the edge, her moans swallowed by his mouth covering hers. She did love him. He could feel it in the way she surrendered, the sound of her voice as she said his name.

Charlie had never been a patient man when it came to the opposite sex. He'd indulged his desires more often than he should have, seeking pleasure that was both immediate and intense. But this was different. With Eve, he felt as if they were moving toward something much bigger and better than the next great orgasm.

He pushed up and looked into her pretty face. Eve smiled and Charlie chuckled. "Yeah, I know. We solve all our problems with sex."

"I guess it works," Eve said.

"Then you're not angry with me?"

"No," Eve said.

"Maybe we should try talking about it?" Charlie said. That's what two people were supposed to do if they had a disagreement. It seemed like a logical suggestion.

Eve groaned. "No. I just want to curl up beside you, close my eyes and sleep for the next twelve hours."

Charlie stood, then drew the covers back. When she'd crawled beneath them, he joined her, pulling her naked body into the curve of his. Resting his chin on her shoulder, he drew a deep breath, then let it out slowly. If there was a perfect spot in all the world, this would have to be it.

Forget mountaintops or beaches or rainforests, forget deserts or canyons or the open ocean. Here, in his bed, with Eve in his arms, he was home. And home was the most perfect place he could imagine.

EVE YAWNED as she scooped freshly ground coffee into the filter basket. She pushed the basket in then flipped the switch, waiting for the coffee to begin trickling into the mug she'd set where the pot belonged.

Charlie was still sound asleep—last night completely exhausted him. But even though Eve wanted to sleep, she couldn't. All night, her mind had whirled with confusion. She'd come to Charlie's house to tell him that she wanted a future with him. But in the end, she couldn't bring herself to do anything but tear off her clothes and allow him to seduce her.

What did that say about the depth of her feelings? That instead of honest conversation, they always resorted to sex? She'd talk to him this morning and clear the air. In between fitful bouts of sleep, she'd managed to formulate a plan, one that didn't put her heart at risk but offered the chance at a real relationship.

Eve grabbed the mug when it was nearly full, then shoved the pot beneath the stream of coffee. She dumped a spoonful of sugar into the mug, then added milk, preparing it exactly the way Charlie preferred.

She grabbed a peanut butter cookie from the jar on the counter and stuck it in her mouth, then walked back to the bedroom. Charlie hadn't moved since she'd left him, his naked body tangled in the sheets, a long, muscular leg hanging off the edge of the bed.

Eve sat down, then gently shook his shoulder. He moaned softly, then opened his eyes and stared up at her. "Are you really waking me up?" he murmured.

"I am," she said, taking the cookie from her mouth. "I need to talk to you."

"Is that coffee for me?"

Eve nodded. "The cookie, too."

"Cookies for breakfast?" He pushed up on his elbow and took the coffee mug from her hand. "What would the food police say?"

"Since these cookies aren't made with refined sugar, the food police would give you a pass. They're better than a lot of other breakfast choices."

Charlie took a bite of the cookie and grinned sleepily. "Maybe this is why the sex is so good. I've been eating nutritious meals. Just think of how good it could be if I started eating tofu. I could go all night long."

Eve laughed. "No tofu for you. I have to sleep sometime."

He set the mug down on the bedside table, then

reached out and ran his finger beneath her eye. "You look tired. I shouldn't keep you up so late. Tonight, I promise, we'll go to bed as soon as you get home from the restaurant. And we'll go to sleep."

"I'm all right," Eve said. "I was up last night thinking...about us."

"Why don't I like the sound of that?" Charlie said, his expression shifting from playful to concerned.

"I've made some decisions. About us." She paused for moment to collect her thoughts, then shook her head. "No, I should explain first."

"Explain what?"

"I haven't told you much about my family. In fact, we haven't spent a lot of time talking about the details of our lives."

"We have time for that," Charlie said.

"Now is the time. I want to tell you about my parents' marriage. And maybe you'll understand why this is so difficult for me." Eve tucked her legs beneath the T-shirt she wore, resting her chin on her knees, her arms wrapped around her shins. "My father was a philanderer. He used to cheat on my mother all the time. Maybe he still does, I don't know. For a long time, she didn't know. Even after I found out, she still didn't know. My father used to take me out to the park on Saturday mornings and I'd play on the swings while he'd sit on a park bench with some woman, having coffee. At first, I thought she was just some mom at the playground with her kids. But then, I realized that she was there to meet him."

Charlie reached out and smoothed his palm over her shoulder. "Eve, I'm sorry."

"Once I'd figured it out, my father just assumed I'd help him keep his secrets. Which I did, because I was afraid if I told my mother, she'd want to divorce him. And even though he was doing this, I still loved him. By the time I was ten, I was helping to hide the evidence. I'd go into his coat pockets and pick out the credit card receipts before my mother found them. I'd throw out the matchbooks from the bars and phone numbers scribbled on scraps of paper. Then one day, my mother caught me doing this and I thought it was all over."

"What happened?"

"I think it was the first time she knew for sure. She might have suspected, but at that point, she knew. She told me not to mention this to my father and to go on as if nothing was wrong. And I did."

"For how long?"

"I was an active enabler until I was thirteen. I begged my father to stop seeing other women, we got in a huge fight, and after that, he stopped for a while. But then it all started again and I did what my mother did. I looked the other way."

"And when your husband cheated on you?"

"I just couldn't do it. I couldn't ignore it. Nor could I ever trust him again."

"And you can't trust me, can you?"

She turned her gaze away, staring out the window. "I want to. I really do. You don't know how much." Eve turned back to him, gathering her resolve. Though she might be taking the biggest risk in her life, Eve was ready to open her heart to him. "I need time. We need time. You seem to know exactly how you feel, but I can't trust how I feel."

"I can give you time," he said. "I have plenty of that. As long as you want. I'll be here for you."

"No," Eve said. "I want you to take the job. We both need to work. In case this doesn't happen for us."

"You can't think that from the start," Charlie said. "You have to believe in us."

"I believe in the us that's here right now. And I believe there might be an us in a month and maybe a year. But this—everything we've shared in this bedroom and in this house, and a few other places, too—that's a fantasy. We have to start to live in the real world."

"I don't want the job," he said. "I don't want to go back to Everest again. I've just barely recovered from the first trip."

"It's a wonderful opportunity. You said so yourself. And I'll miss you when you're gone. But you'll come back. This time, I know you'll be back."

Charlie searched her face, as if he were hoping to find a trace of uncertainty there, a chink in her logic. This was for the best, Eve mused. He had to see it the way she did. If they continued as they'd begun, the fantasy would slowly fade and they'd be left wondering if the emotions that accompanied it were fading, too. This way, they'd force themselves back into reality, before it was too late.

"All right," Charlie said. "I'll do whatever it takes. I won't always like it, but I'll do what you want."

"And if you're not happy, you'll tell me. You won't sneak around with other women, you'll just tell me so we can end it without any drama."

"It's not going to end," Charlie said.

Eve grabbed the coffee mug from the beside table and took a sip. "I spoke with Lily about your idea. About the dehydrated foods. She's doing some research, but she thought it was a really good idea."

"It is," Charlie said. "Listen, I've tasted every brand out there and there just isn't much variety. The food needs to taste…interesting. And it has to be packed with carbs."

"I'm going to work on some things while you're gone," Eve said. Though the words were difficult to say and even more difficult to imagine, Eve knew she'd be able to get along without him. A month was a long time. Six weeks even worse. But it would never come close to five years.

"I don't know what I'm going to do without you," he said.

"You'll be fine."

"You could always come along," Charlie said. "We'll spend a lot of time at base camp and you'll get a chance to see how the cooking is done there. The Sherpas are amazing cooks. They do a lot of vegetarian dishes. You could get some new recipes."

"I can't be away from the restaurant for that long," Eve said.

"Why not? A lot of great chefs travel. And Asia is a great place to study food."

Eve had always wanted to experience the culinary world beyond the borders of her own country. She had the money to travel, but there always seemed to be something important keeping her home. "Maybe another time. Things are so busy right now with the investors and the new restaurant in Seattle and the cookbook and the television show. And Nepal isn't just a quick plane ride with a comfy hotel on the other end. It takes planning."

"All right," Charlie said. "But you do have to promise me one thing. That when I get back, we'll take a trip together. Just a long weekend. Anywhere you want to go. San Francisco. New Orleans. Some place with really great food. And we'll eat our way through the weekend."

Eve smiled. It sounded like a perfect plan. Something she could look forward to upon his return. "All right," she agreed.

For the first time, she allowed herself to believe they had a future. He would come back to Boulder, they would pick up where they'd left off. And maybe, someday, she could say without a trace of hesitation that she loved Charlie Templeton with every fiber of her being, with every molecule in her body and every inch of her soul.

THE DENVER AIRPORT was bustling with travelers as Eve and Charlie wove through the crowd on the way to his gate. Though Eve had known this moment was coming, she found herself completely unprepared for the emotions that accompanied it. Charlie was leaving for Boston and a few days later, he'd be on a plane bound for Nepal. He'd be halfway around the world and difficult to reach.

In the week before his departure, their relationship had continued to edge toward something permanent. She packed up her things at Lily's and moved into his house, hanging her clothes beside his in the empty closets and filling his kitchen cupboards with all of her cooking utensils and spices.

Though the house had been furnished as a rental, Charlie had urged her to buy new furniture and redecorate while he was gone. He'd brought his friend Jack over to discuss the changes she wanted to make in the kitchen and Jack had agreed to help her find a good contractor.

But Eve hadn't wanted to think about redecorating. She'd only been interested in knowing where he'd be, what he'd be doing and whether any of it was dangerous. Charlie had tried to calm her fears and to that end, had decided to set up an easy way for them to communicate on a daily basis.

He had a satellite link-up on his laptop, so he'd gone out and bought a brand-new computer and set it up in a corner of his living room, along with a program that operated a video link over the Internet. They'd first tried it with Charlie locked in the bedroom and Eve sitting in the living room.

When the link-up worked, they explored all the possibilities that video calling offered, including those of a sexual nature. Eve felt a blush warm her cheeks. Though sex in the privacy of their bedroom was comfortable for her, she had a difficult time sending images of her naked body out into the world.

"You're going to call me as soon as you get to Boston, right?" Eve said.

"I will," Charlie said. "Are you sure you don't want to come to Boston with me? It's just a few days. You could fly out there with me now and fly back here when I leave for Nepal."

"I can't," Eve said. "I have to go to Seattle the day after tomorrow to look at a few locations for the restaurant. I'm cooking for my investors and then I have to spend a few days here in Denver, talking to a production company about the cooking show."

"See, you'll be so busy, you'll hardly notice I'm gone. Six weeks will fly by in no time."

Eve stood next to him as he checked in and

dropped off his luggage. They wandered over to a row of seats, then sat down. Charlie reached out to take her hand. He drew it up to his lips and pressed a kiss on the back of her wrist. "God, I'm going to miss you."

"I'll miss you, too," she said. A shiver skittered through her body and she glanced away. She'd been meaning to talk to Charlie about something before he left, but she hadn't had the courage to bring up the subject. It was now or never.

"Will there be women where you're going in Nepal?"

He frowned. "Sure. There are a lot of women involved in climbing expeditions. The season will be winding down on Everest. Why do you—" He paused, then smiled. "Are you worried I'm going to...what do they call it?"

"Stray," Eve said. "Because, I know you're used to having women around to satisfy—your—you know, needs?" Charlie laughed out loud and Eve felt her face warm. "It's not funny. I'm serious."

"You're ridiculous. You don't think I can go six weeks without sex?"

"Have you ever gone six weeks without sex?" she asked. "I mean, during your adult life?"

Charlie thought about it. "No, I guess I haven't. But that doesn't mean I can't." He grabbed Eve's arms and turned her to face him. "Eve, listen to me very carefully. I want you and only you. I'm not going to go sleeping around just to scratch an itch. You are the only person I want to be intimate with, do you understand?"

Eve nodded. "I do."

"Good. Now, can we stop talking about sex? It's making me really horny and finding a place to take care of my needs in this airport is going to be impossible."

"See," Eve said. "You get turned on so easily. I think it's going to be much harder than you think."

"It is much harder than you think," Charlie said, glancing down at his lap. "But that's all your fault. You're the one who does this to me. That's why I set up the video link on your computer. So we could take care of these things when they come…up." He sat up straighter, wincing slightly as he moved. "Now, can we talk about something else? Tell me about the new sofa you want to buy."

Eve chatted about her plans to redecorate the house, promising him that she'd clear all her choices with him. But she knew the conversation was just a clever way to distract her from the inevitable.

Charlie looked at his watch, then sighed. "I'd better go. I still have to go through security." He took her hand and gave it a squeeze.

Eve swallowed hard as his gaze caught hers. "Right," she muttered. "I guess this is it."

"It's all right, Evie. We'll say goodbye really quick.

And before you know it, you'll be here again, picking me up."

"You are coming back," Eve said.

Charlie stood and pulled her to her feet. "I am coming back. I promise." He leaned forward and kissed her, this kiss filled with so much longing that Eve felt tears well up in her eyes.

"Have fun," she said, her voice choking with emotion. "But—but not too much fun. Not that kind of fun."

"Evie, don't you know? I love you. The only person I want to be with is you." He reached down and picked up his boarding pass and passport. "I'll talk to you later tonight after I get settled in Boston."

Eve nodded. "All right." She grabbed his hand and gave it a squeeze, then realized she didn't want to let go. "Go. Before I start blubbering like an idiot."

"I can't," Charlie said. "You're holding on too tight."

Eve quickly released her grip. Brushing a tear from her cheek, she gave him a little wave and he started toward the gate. Eve felt panic wash over her. What if she never saw him again? What if he met with an accident on Everest or his plane crashed or—he met some beautiful woman and decided to run off with her? There were things left to be said between them.

"I love you, Charlie Templeton," Eve shouted.

He stopped, then slowly turned around, a wide

grin on his face. "I love you, Eve Keller." They stared at each other across the waiting area for a long moment. Then applause suddenly broke out among the passengers standing there.

Eve laughed and blew him a kiss and Charlie pretended to catch it and put it in his pocket. He gave her one last wave before heading into the security area.

Walking back toward her car, Eve said a silent prayer that everything would go well with his trip and he'd make it safely home again. This man meant everything to her. Though she found those feelings difficult to admit, that didn't make them any less intense.

"I do love you, Charlie," she murmured.

9

"HEY, CHARLIE! YOU HAVE a visitor!"

Charlie glanced up from his laptop and groaned. He'd been at base camp for a week and already he'd garnered a reputation. Most of the guys there called him "whipped." A few used the word "obsessed." It was only the women who showed the slightest bit of admiration for his chaste ways and his devotion to his girlfriend back home.

Sure, he spent a lot of time on the computer. When he and Eve couldn't get a video link, they wrote each other long letters, detailing all the things they'd done that day. And when the video link was working, Charlie shut himself up in his tent and enjoyed the pleasures of Internet sex.

At first, Eve had been a bit embarrassed, but as time went on, she looked forward to their "inter-ludes." A week ago, she'd showed off a sexy new bra and panties, which were slowly peeled off before getting down to business.

Charlie had been adventurous in the bedroom in the past, but he'd never experienced this kind of sex. Without the ability to touch her, everything happened in his head. The orgasms were at times incredibly intense and at other times, almost soothing.

"Templeton!"

"Go away," Charlie said.

He'd been in a bitch of a mood the past five days. He hadn't been able to reach Eve in more than a week and he was beginning to worry. She'd sent him a short note saying she was going to be traveling and might not have access to a computer for a while. Charlie found it a bit odd that she couldn't find a single computer in an entire week.

He'd decided to call the restaurant and find out where she was if he didn't hear from her by the end of the day. It was easy to let his thoughts run away on him, especially when they were so far apart. Maybe she met another man. Maybe Matt was romancing her again. Or maybe she'd just lost interest.

Charlie watched as a shadow crossed in front of his tent. "Don't think this is going to work again," he shouted.

Yesterday, some old friends from an American expedition had decided to play a joke on him. They'd told him they were sending a girl over to his tent to help him out with his "problem." Though sex at base camp, or anywhere on Everest, was considered taboo by the locals, most of the climbers didn't abstain when the opportunity presented itself.

But when Charlie stepped out of his tent, he had found a huge blow-up doll, mouth agape, dressed in a climbing harness and crampons. The entire camp was gathered to see his reaction. Though he took it with good humor, Charlie realized how many people didn't really believe he could be faithful to Eve.

"Just leave the doll," he called. "Stake her to the ground so she doesn't blow away. I'll get her back to you guys later. I know how much you'll miss her."

"Ah, Charlie. I think you better come out here."

With a low curse, he got up from his cot and crossed the spacious interior of his tent. Grabbing the tent flap, he tossed it up and stepped into the bright sunshine. His eyes took a while to adjust to the light and he squinted, holding his hand up to shield them. "I know you think it's funny. Ha-ha. Charlie Templeton has a girlfriend. Charlie Templeton is in love. Go ahead, laugh it up. But don't tell me that if you guys found the perfect woman, you wouldn't do everything in your power to make her happy."

He pulled his hand away from his eyes and saw Mark Eaton standing in front of him, a satisfied smirk curling his lips. "Well, I'm sure she'll be happy to hear that," he said.

"Hi, Charlie."

The sound of her voice sent a jolt of surprise

through his body. At first he wasn't sure if he was imagining what he heard. Charlie slowly turned, then gasped at the sight he found.

Eve, dressed in a hodgepodge of outdoor gear, standing in front of him. In one quick motion, he scooped her up into his arms and kissed her, cupping her face in his hands as his mouth found hers.

When he finally took the opportunity to grab a breath, he looked down into her bright eyes. "What are you doing here?"

"You told me I should come. And I had a few weeks free, so I thought I'd see a little bit of Nepal."

He laughed, then kissed her again. "How did you get here?"

"It wasn't easy," she said. "I called twenty different tour companies before I found one that had a spot open. Luckily, I didn't need a visa, but I did have to get a bunch of shots. I was on a plane for a day and a half. Then I was stuck in Lhasa for two days getting used to the altitude. I spent another day bouncing around in a van. But the trip has been incredible, just like you said it would be. I saw a monastery and I've eaten really incredible food. And if I don't sit down right now, I think I might just fall down."

He pulled aside the tent flap and showed her inside. She glanced around at the spacious interior. They'd set up a comfortable tent for him at base camp with plenty of room to work and sleep. The production company considered him the "star" of their film, and he was happy to be treated as such. Now he realized how lucky it was that he had room for two.

"How are you?" Charlie asked, gently drawing her down to sit on the cot.

"Good," she said. "Tired."

"The altitude can take some getting used to. You'll just be a little breathless or lightheaded for a while. But if you feel sick you should let me—"

She put her finger over his lips. "Aren't you going to tell me how much you missed me?" she teased.

"I missed you a lot," he said, her finger still touching his lips.

"Aren't you going to tell me how good I look?"

Charlie chuckled. "You look really good," he said.

She reached for the zipper of her jacket and slowly drew it down. "Aren't you going to tell me how much you want me?"

Charlie held his breath as she stripped off everything but her bra and panties, the same bra and panties she'd shown him via videophone. "I'll never stop wanting you," he murmured, reaching out to smooth his hand along her thigh. "So, Evie, what exactly does this mean? What did you come all this way to tell me?"

She smiled. "I want a life with you, Charlie. I want you there when I open my new restaurant in Seattle. I want you to taste my recipes for my new cookbook and I want you to stand in the wings while I tape my first show. I want to start our business together. I want to travel to all the places you mentioned and more. We'll eat our way around the world. And I want to—"

Charlie pressed his finger to her lips, then softly shushed her. "Just say it, Evie. Be brave and just say it." He drew his hand away from her face.

"I love you, Charlie."

He knew it was a moment he'd remember for the rest of his life. All the details would come back to him years from now—the wind flapping at the tent, the scent of her hair, the way her skin felt beneath his fingertips. "And I love you, Eve."

"We're going to have a wonderful life together, Charlie," she said. "With lots of adventure. And I think we should start that life right now." She pushed him down on the cot, then crawled on top of him.

"Bring it on," Charlie said with a laugh.

Epilogue

ANGELA WEATHERBY STARED at her computer screen, trying to decide what was wrong with the beginning of the fifth chapter of her book. She'd been doing so well. The Charmer, the Drifter. But now, she'd run up against a wall—and the memory of a man who'd once been the object of all of her most vivid fantasies.

Max Morgan. The most gorgeous man she'd ever met. They'd gone to high school together in Evanston and then attended the same college. And until her junior year at Northwestern, he'd been the only man she'd ever loved—even though it had been from afar.

They'd spoken just once. Angela had been assigned a story for the college newspaper about a "beefcake" calendar that one of the frats was selling to benefit a local charity. Max Morgan had been the subject of the interview. Even after all this time, she couldn't remember a single thing they'd said to each other.

After reviewing her tape, she'd been mortified at how foolish she'd sounded. It was no wonder a guy like Max would have never noticed a girl like her.

Angela sighed softly. Fast-forward five years, to a night that had been burned indelibly into Angela's mind. She'd made a blind date and was scheduled to meet the cousin of a coworker at a popular sports bar. Instead, she'd looked across the bar and found Max Morgan staring at her.

He'd been in town, his team playing a three-game series with the White Sox. He'd been surrounded by women, but he'd looked across the bar and their gazes had met...and held. He'd smiled, a silent invitation for her to come and talk to him. But Angela had been so nervous, she'd turned away. And when she looked back, he'd moved on to another girl.

"The Sexy Devil," she murmured.

She'd always wondered what made a guy like him tick. He could have any woman he wanted. He'd dated models and actresses and heiresses. He'd been on the front covers of men's magazines and the tabloids. Max Morgan was the quintessential bad boy, the kind of guy every woman wanted to tame. If she could get an interview with him for her book, then maybe she'd be able to gain some interesting insights into all smooth operators.

Angela smiled to herself. Wow, she'd really managed to rationalize that. In truth, she was curious. Curious to see if he remembered her. Curious to see if she still felt an attraction to him. Curious to see what kind of man Max had become.

But she'd made a few mistakes trying to get interviews for some of the earlier chapters in her book. She'd never been able to connect with Alex Stamos. Constant phone calls hadn't worked. So she'd decided to try a more aggressive approach with Charlie Templeton, tracking him down in Boulder. But that hadn't worked either.

This time, Angela was going to try a bit of subterfuge. If Max had been attracted to her once, then maybe he'd be attracted again. She'd just have to find a way to meet him. She picked up an invitation she'd received recently for a charity event sponsored by a Chicago Children's Hospital.

"Hosted by major leaguers Max Morgan and Kirk Caldwell," she said to herself. She knew exactly where he'd be in two weeks. And she planned to be there, too.

"You will not believe this," Ceci said, poking her head in Angela's office door. "I just got a note from a woman who wrote a profile for our site and she and the guy she profiled are moving in together. And guess who the guy is?"

"Considering we have tens of thousands of profiles on our site, that's going to be a bit difficult."

"You've met him," she hinted.

"Max Morgan?"

"No!" Ceci cried. "Wait. You know Max Morgan?"

"No," Angela lied. "Well, I know of him. I don't know him like...you know..."

"Charlie Templeton," Ceci said. "The guy you tried to interview out in Colorado. I guess he's ready to settle down and this woman wants us to take the profile down."

"What did you say?"

"I said we could take her comments down but the others would stay up."

"What did she say?"

"She said fine and hung up."

Angela leaned back in her chair, staring up at the ceiling. "This is weird. I try to interview both these guys and they've both suddenly found the perfect women. What are the odds of that?"

"I guess it just proves my point," Ceci said. "Even though you don't want to believe it, men can change."

Angela looked at her friend and business partner. "Maybe," she murmured.

After Ceci left the room, Angela returned to her computer, staring for a long moment at her manuscript. Then, she opened her favorite search engine and typed in Max Morgan's name. A photo of him escorting a famous model to dinner came up first.

"You're next, Max Morgan. If I've suddenly got the power to turn smooth operators into devoted partners, then I'm coming for you next."

* * * * *

Shaw cursed and hooked his arm around Sabrina.

Despite the urgency that the deadly gunfire created, he tried to be careful with her, and he took the brunt of the fall when he pulled her to the ground. His shoulder hit hard, but he held on tight to his gun so that it wouldn't be jarred from his hand.

Shaw didn't stop there. He crawled over Sabrina, sheltering her pregnant belly with his body, and he came up ready to return fire.

This was obviously a situation he'd wanted to avoid at all cost. He didn't want his baby in the middle of a fight with these armed fugitives, but when they fired that shot, they'd left him no choice. Now, the trick was to get Sabrina safely out of there.

"Get down," someone on the SWAT team yelled from the roof of the adjacent building.

Shaw did. He dropped lower, covering Sabrina as best he could.

There was another shot, but this one came from a rifleman on the SWAT team. Shaw didn't look up, but he heard the sound of glass being blown apart.

The shots continued, all coming from his men, which meant it might be time to try to get Sabrina to better cover. Shaw glanced at the front of the building.

So that Sabrina's pregnant belly wouldn't be smashed against the ground, Shaw eased off her and moved her to a sitting position so that her back was against the brick wall. They were close. Too close. And face-to-face.

He found himself staring right into those sea-green eyes.

How will Shaw get Sabrina out?
Follow the daring rescue and the heartbreaking
aftermath in THE BABY'S GUARDIAN
by Delores Fossen, available May 2010 from
Harlequin Intrigue.

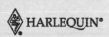

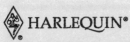

HARLEQUIN®

LAURA MARIE ALTOM

The Baby Twins

Stephanie Olmstead has her hands full raising
her twin baby girls on her own. When she runs
into old friend Brady Flynn, she's shocked to find
herself suddenly attracted to the handsome airline
pilot! Will this flyboy be the perfect daddy—
or will he crash and burn?

Babies
&
Bachelors
USA

"LOVE, HOME & HAPPINESS"

www.eHarlequin.com

HAR7536

Former bad boy Sloan Hawkins is back in
Redemption, Oklahoma, to help keep his aunt's
cherished garden thriving and to reconnect with the
girl he left behind, Annie Markham. But when he
discovers his secret child—and that single mother
Annie never stopped loving him—he's determined
that a wedding will take place in the garden
nurtured by faith and love.

Where healing flows...

Look for

The Wedding Garden
by Linda Goodnight

Available May 2010
wherever you buy books.

Steeple
Hill®
LI87595

HARLEQUIN® *Blaze*™

is proud to introduce...

New York Times bestselling author

Brenda Jackson

with
SPONTANEOUS

Kim Cannon and Duan Jeffries have a great thing going.
Whenever they meet up, the passion between them
is hot, intense…spontaneous. And things really heat
up when Duan agrees to accompany her to her
mother's wedding. Too bad there's something
he's not telling her.…

Don't miss the fireworks!

*Available in May 2010
wherever Harlequin Blaze books are sold.*

---

red-hot reads